MAKE YOUR MOVE
And Other Stories

By the same author:

THE BULL LEAPERS
THE FREEDOM TREE
LEGION OF THE WHITE TIGER
SIGN OF THE SWALLOW
TALKING IN WHISPERS
WHERE NOBODY SEES

MAKE YOUR MOVE
And Other Stories

James Watson

LONDON
VICTOR GOLLANCZ LTD
1988

In memory of Barry Taylor (1936–1987)

First published in Great Britain 1988
by Victor Gollancz Ltd,
14 Henrietta Street, London WC2E 8QJ

Copyright © 1988 by James Watson

British Library Cataloguing in Publication Data
Watson, James, *1936*–
  Make your move and other stories.
  I. Title
  823'.914[J]

ISBN 0-575-04397-0

Photoset in Great Britain by
Rowland Phototypesetting Ltd, Bury St Edmunds, Suffolk
and printed by St Edmundsbury Press Ltd,
Bury St Edmunds, Suffolk

Contents

The Eyes Have It	7
Make Your Move	13
Tom Bleeding Who?	28
This Nothing Will Never End	47
Smiley	63
Choices	69
Sir Les Of The Windmills	90
The Rebellion of the Names	124
The Great Tattoo	146

The Eyes Have It

The little girl who has come up the steps of the double-decker stares at Gina. It is a stare of such penetrating hatred that, for a moment, Gina holds her gaze as if doing so might reveal some mistake. But the girl's stare is for her. Its withering concentration is for her.

The child kneels on the seat in front of Gina, and facing her. She presses herself against the backrest, gripping the chrome frame with tight fingers.

Do I know you, and yet have somehow forgotten? Gina cannot remember ever seeing this child before. The face is oval and pale. It is sharp, stretched; harshly pretty. Her eyes burn. I hate you. I detest you. There is no doubt about their message.

You are sixteen, Gina reminds herself. This child is eight, maybe nine. This is a game. Sensible sixteen year olds know better than to play games with strangers, even this young.

You've got to be careful what you do with your eyes. So the book said. Not this book in Gina's hands, page half read, but the book on how you say things—say so much—without speaking; without words.

It's a tease. Look away.

Gina resumes her reading. She is disturbed. She feels the gaze of the child, its hostility, ramming at her lowered eyelids, piercing them. Read. Concentrate. This could be good practice. The story is about a soldier returning from war. His face has been burnt away by an incendiary bomb. He is unrecognisable. He enters a Scottish seaport as dusk falls. His lover lives at the end cottage overlooking the harbour wall.

Gina reassures herself. It is the story which is making you tense, not this child. You are anticipating how the soldier's beautiful girl will respond as she looks upon her faceless lover. It is a test. Yes, for the reader as well as the girl.

Turning the page, Gina looks up and meets once more the face of the child—staring, staring. Right at you, right into you. It is on the tip of her tongue to say, 'Do you mind not staring?' Should I break the ice, crack a joke and crack the stare? No. Silence is best. Little girls ought not to talk to strangers, even to bigger girls who feel intimidated by them.

No one is safe these days. Dad said. Mum says, Absolutely no one. Whatever happened to kindness? And remember the eyes.

It seems to be the end of the incident, for the girl's mother, who has been paying the fares below, comes up from the lower deck. Same hard face, but thankfully eyes that are not staring. She wears a heavy full-length coat despite the summer heat. Worn, thinks Gina. A worn-out person. Her handbag is not properly closed.

"There," she says, dropping down on to the seat beside her daughter. It is almost amusing, for she bounces down, as if she too enjoys a game. "All set, eh?"

The child turns on one knee, reluctant to surrender her incursion into Gina's private space. She leans towards her mother as if to touch heads. Gina is about to read again, but holds off a moment as the child immediately raises her hand as a barricade and begins to whisper in her mother's ear. She does it brazenly, all the while staring—staring and staring—at Gina.

Whispering. Long and feverishly. About me.

She ponders, How can you be so afraid?—of a mere child, on a bus in the middle of a sunlit day. Don't be stupid. Read. The faceless soldier has reached the end-terrace house. Rain sweeps in from the sea. Cold, stabbing rain. It runs across the scars where his eyebrows had been.

A gas lamp at the street corner betrays without mercy his red injuries.

It is the wrong time to come. It is the witching hour; but the stubbornness within him will have it no other way. He has borne his injury too long alone.

"Well if she does that again, there'll be trouble." The mother's voice is no whisper. She has turned her head only a fraction, but the words have been unmistakenly cast behind her at Gina; in a tone of warning.

And the message continues. The words pour into the receptive ear. "Is that so? Is that so then?" Now a glance around. "Oh." A stare: the burning stare. "Is that so?" Quite aloud. Don't the others on the bus hear? "She did? Well just this once more, believe me."

Gina shifts her own gaze as if it were something heavy, which suddenly needed manoeuvring like furniture. Lifting it, heaving it from the page; angling it away from the nodding head of the mother, the child's tireless insolence.

Gina forces her eyes to scan the faces of the other passengers. If they have noticed anything they have decided against bearing witness.

Cardboard cut-outs. The book had said, The soldier's eyes were dark holes, empty. Yours too, thought Gina. She recalled the experience of being a tiny child: if you did not want a thing to exist, you averted your eyes. When you grow up, the trick no longer works.

But for the passengers it is a comfort.

Gina tries their route of escape. She looks out on to the passing landscape, of green hills whose sides erosion has ripped away to reveal naked chalk; different from the rolling woodland the bus has just passed through. Gina's brother had once called it Rupert Bear country.

This isn't a Rupert Bear story, thinks Gina. I wish it was.

"Is that so?" That phrase again. This time the mother swings round on full shoulder. She stares at Gina: the same eyes as her child, the same venom. Now two pairs of eyes swallow the space between passengers who have never met before.

Gina raises her book almost to the level of her face. It could be construed as a provocative action, but she does not look up to note the effect upon the conspirators.

Yes, she is defining them as that. It is a plot. To pick on someone. Perhaps anyone.

"And she needn't think that'll make any difference."

Though the page of the book is nearer, the words are blurred. Your hand is shaking. You cannot hold it at this level and stop it shaking.

Read!

The soldier's knock has sounded in the night. He waits. The rain has flattened his hair upon his skull; his clothes have shrunk about his limbs. He is enough to scare the dead.

Gina attempts to counter the words on the page: Rupert Bear, Rupert Bear; safe and smiling in red jersey and yellow check pants.

Read!

"We'll do something about it, don't fret."

Read! But what's this fiction compared to these characters one arm's reach away? Gina thinks, maybe fiction is what happens to other people. This mother and her kid want me dead. It is in their eyes. I have become something for them. Perhaps I remind them of somebody who once did them harm.

As if in recognition of her hysteria, and to subdue it by meeting it head on, Gina looks up swiftly.

"There!"

And the mother echoes the child, loud enough for the whole bus to hear. "Sure, love, sure!"

Again, whispering.

I do not know you.

Read. It is probably all in your imagination.

The whisper has no end. It grows on itself, issuing coils out of nothing.

In the story, the door of the end-terrace cottage has

opened on to darkness—and eyes; not of the young woman as the soldier expects, but of a dog springing from the recesses of the room.

Yet thank God. The bus is coming to a stop—their stop, mother and child. The girl refuses Gina the blessing of her back, of her retreat. She stands, turns, stares. She challenges Gina to look; forces her to look.

The shock of the eyes is as intense as it is unjust: why me? And the face that frames the eyes is grizzled, an old woman's face, like those swathed in black shawls they show of Lebanon after the bombs, after the bodies have strewn the city pavements; after the incendiaries have burnt the victims out of recognition.

Eyes accusing the whole world.

The mother has reached the steps. She descends. The girl has waited her moment. The bus mirror reflects the mother's journey. The girl faces Gina.

"We know who *you* are!"

The girl thrusts out her tongue. A snake, skin-shorn, a quivering spear of a tongue. Then she follows her mother down.

The relief is immense. It's over. It's happened to me alone, though up here I'm not alone. Gina takes in the faces of her fellow passengers. Has even one of you noticed, heard? How would they come forward if obliged?

There's never no smoke without fire, my dear.

She heads back into her book and she finds she has turned two pages at once. It is not the end of the story. Already sensing this, Gina is peering into the round bus mirror which gives a perfect view of the child and her mother on the bus platform. And the child is pointing upwards; up the steps.

Read. Blank out. The bus can't be stopped for ever. The dog has sprung in joyful recognition of the soldier. It is a blind love. The soldier stumbles and the stair passage is all at once filled with the mother returning. In her fury, scrambling up.

The eyes have it.

She is tall and advancing on Gina. She does not hesitate. She strikes Gina in the face. Advances, strikes her, the back of her hand to Gina's cheek and bone, then again with the fingers taut, nails out, she lands a blow downwards and across.

The woman does not speak until she has finished her assault. She is a tower over Gina. "And don't you do that again, Miss, to a girl who's been in hospital . . . You slut!"

Gina partially deflects a final blow that sends her book skating along the bus floor. "I never . . ."

The woman wheels about. She spares one glance at the passengers. "Our day out," she cries. "And this happens!" She goes down the stairs to her daughter. Together, they alight from the bus.

Gina does not move. She leaves her book on the floor. She feels the eyes now; their interest, their unspoken accusations. Her face stings, but she will not touch it. She will not acknowledge wounds, not yet, though she may be bleeding and her neck feels ricked.

Cardboard cut-outs. She will not give them that satisfaction. She recovers her book. There is going to be a happy ending, of a sort. Gina reads. She shakes.

Forget it.

A case of . . .

Be cardboard, like them. It helps. But her whole body is trembling. She watches, helpless, as a tear falls on to the page. For a split second the tear magnifies the letters beneath it as the bus mirror magnified the angry mother. Between them, the tear and the dark print form the pupil of a glaring eye.

For Sophie, to whom something very like this actually happened.

Make Your Move

"That is what I said, Mr Spicer—behaving in a peculiar manner. Quite peculiar and most inappropriate."

It surprised John Spicer, head of the Neighbourhood Community Scheme, that Madeleine Rudge had been described in such words. She was such a silent one; a plain Jane, who did what she was told and never stepped out of line.

Spicer was also amused by this report on the young lady in her second week of a Placement at the Refuge of the Holy Saints Mary and Joseph.

They were all peculiar at that place. It was why they were there. Peculiar behaviour, mused John Spicer, was what Madeleine's Placement was all about.

"Has she not done her jobs properly, Matron?"

"Oh yes. In that sense she's the best girl you've ever sent us. The place has never been cleaner. She never forgets their morning coffee, afternoon tea, evening cocoa—who takes sugar, who doesn't . . . But Mr Spicer, she's filling our men's heads with utter nonsense. At least, more nonsense than they've got already."

In the first place, John Spicer had not been happy at sending teenage girls into a rest home for ageing men whose families had given up on them. But placements were in short supply, and Madeleine had actually shown enthusiasm when he had suggested the idea.

Enthusiasm! In this job, to find a kid with enthusiasm was like stumbling over a crock of gold. "I like old people," Madeleine had said. "My granddad was a treasure."

"But these are . . . er, senile, Maddy. Fuddled. Their families can't cope, or they're just friendless. They wander about all day in pyjamas, stare at the ceiling, catch flies. In short, they're not normal."

"My granddad wasn't normal. He wet the bed and the floor and—"

"Okay, Maddy, spare me the grisly details."

"But up to the end he told right good stories."

Stories were what Matron complained Madeleine was telling. "What kind of stories, Matron?" But Matron was too busy to explain over the phone.

"This afternoon would be best for your visit, Mr Spicer. After tea and before bathtime."

Bathtime at five in the afternoon? No wonder they were all crackers. John Spicer had got out Madeleine's documents: family of seven; father went to find work in Germany, never returned; those over sixteen years of age, all unemployed; one boy in a remand centre; the mother addicted to sherry and depression.

Nothing peculiar about that. Not for this district, where harrowing family problems were as common as wet summers.

No mention of a granddad.

John Spicer did not disturb the concentration of the two chess players as he entered the recreation room at the Refuge through a white-gleaming, fine-panelled door. The room retained a shabby elegance. Its ceiling was richly moulded and there was a black marble fireplace inlaid with coloured glass.

Madeleine Rudge sat with her back to a casement window. The rays of the late afternoon sun seemed to filter through her. Though they dimmed her features they traced a dazzling line around her head and shoulders and along her bare forearm covered with the lightest fleece of hair, settling finally on the White Knight held between her forefinger and thumb.

"That is our Mr Nelson," said Matron, remaining at the door. "And, well, you know Madeleine."

Not this Madeleine, thought Spicer. She's, well—quite

changed. Transfigured. From lacklustre plainness to this radiance; beautiful, even.

There are always surprises in this job.

"Chess is a great favourite with Mr Nelson," Matron was explaining. "Isn't that right, Mr Nelson?"

Mr Nelson was too absorbed in the game to reply. He wore a brown dressing gown. He had slipped bare feet from orange flip-flops and was gently rubbing the ball of his foot against the shin of his other leg. His head tilted sideways on a long, scraggy neck. He did not look round.

"And he is a little on the deaf side," added Matron as if to explain Mr Nelson's indifference to the arrival of the newcomer. "If it's all right, I'll leave you to it. There's a bell push if you need me."

This was John Spicer's first visit to the Refuge of the Holy Saints Mary and Joseph: a quiet city street west of the port road; plane trees along the pavements, heavily pruned; a winding path through privet hedges and shrubbery. The lawns of the Refuge were populated with statues of angels in white marble and saints with bronze haloes which had dribbled green stain into their hair.

Like giant white jelly babies, thought John Spicer. And among the trees stood living statues, the forlorn shapes of residents who had braved the autumn chill to escape from the house.

More dead than alive, poor sods. How do you look mad just by standing? John Spicer shuddered. Not angels or jelly babies, but old crocks. The ornate entrance hall, with marble arches, marble floors and a high-domed ceiling dampened his spirits even further. Abandon hope all ye that enter here.

Confronting him in an alcove beneath the extravagant staircase was the statue of Sir Oliver Peabody, Victorian benefactor, whose wealth had paid for these cold stones. In one hand he bore a scroll of mayoral office with a seal of the city dangling on marble silk; in the other he held a model of one of his many iron ships that steamed the oceans of the world.

"Probably made his first million," John Spicer heard himself say half-aloud, "in the slave trade." This lordly pile, he decided, must represent conscience money. He scanned the gold lettering on the plinth. The house had not originally been bequeathed for the support of senile old men in pyjamas, but for the sustenance of gentlewomen who had fallen upon hard times.

The angels in marble, the old men in feeble flesh and Oliver Peabody in his arrogance lingered in John Spicer's mind as he watched Maddy and her chess partner, Mr Nelson. The documents picturesquely described the old man as Madeleine Rudge's 'case study'. Her duty was not only to dress, wash, shave and feed him, Maddy had to keep case notes on him and eventually write a report.

All part of the Scheme.

First there had been the angels, now Maddy. Set against the light, she took on the image of the Holy Mother, a mixture of shadow and iridescence; like a painting on the high altar of a cathedral. John Spicer did not normally fancy girls on the Scheme, but the calmness and the stillness of this girl—her monumentality—ruffled his senses.

He was at once admiring and uneasy. "Afternoon, Maddy."

"Afternoon, Mr Spicer."

"Will you introduce me?"

"Mr Nelson—he's a racing driver."

"Ah."

The old man grinned, toothless. There were sores on his hand and the wrist seemed so fragile that John Spicer was careful with his handshake in case something snapped.

"She's writing a book about me, you know. My biographer, you might say."

"Is that right, Maddy?"

Mr Nelson explained: "I've told her my secrets. About my time with the Royal Family. My service with the

King of Jordan. I fought with John Wayne in the Korean War, you know. It's going to be a best seller. Tell him what we're going to do with the money, Maddy, my pet."

"Take a slow boat to China."

"Hong Kong. I'm going to show her the sights. Where the flying fishes play. Wonderful. And the sun comes up like thunder. I'm known in Hong Kong. The police there owe me a favour or two, I'll tell you."

"Very sticky in Hong Kong," said John Spicer, all the while staring at Maddy who, in her cocoon of shadow, remained as still as the chess pieces in front of her.

"Not in the lagoons," she replied. "Under the palm trees, with the ocean washing your ankles, like."

"And all the tequila you can drink," added Mr Nelson. He gestured at the chess board. "Play, girl, make your move!"

Looking at Madeleine as she languidly placed her knight in the centre of the board, John Spicer sensed not only beauty but an emanation of power. It was a deliberately reckless move which Mr Nelson pounced on with a crow of delight. He fumbled with a pawn and drove Maddy's white knight clean off the board. "Champion! Well, what's the reward for that canny little move, our Maddy?"

Madeleine took her time to answer. "It's only when you checkmate me that you get your reward."

"But what will it be, Maddy—tell me!" Mr Nelson did his own explaining. He swivelled round to face John Spicer. "We'll be at the captain's table. There'll be champagne breakfasts. There'll be filmstars, right, Maddy?"

"They'll not let you on the captain's table in your flip-flops, Mr Nelson."

Mr Nelson grinned. "Her Dad, you see—he owns Cunard, the liner people."

Madeleine's hand was white and trim above the next sacrificial piece, Queen's bishop.

Matron had said, "To us normal people, Madeleine's

fantasies are just adolescent dreams. But not to our residents."

Mr Nelson was saying, "It's not a well-known fact about me that I'm the fastest man on earth. That's how I lost my sight. They had to put me in here. My wife'll tell you. Too fast for the world. Fastest runner, fastest eater, fastest lover. Nobody in this world ever drove faster than me. I had this lorry—and that's how it happened, why my wife divorced me. I was doing the motorway at over a hundred and fifty when I suddenly went blind. One minute I could see, the next—nothing!"

How he escaped death, said Mr Nelson, was one of his two great secrets. Only Maddy knew them. "Right, pet?"

"Right, Mr Nelson."

"They call me Speedy Gonzales."

Mr Nelson stared at John Spicer with watery blue eyes. He tapped his nose. "Two secrets."

Spicer was for getting away from this madhouse; or I'll begin to doubt my own sanity. The misgivings he had about sending innocent teenagers into places such as this were confirmed.

We've no right to do this to them. Not just to keep them off the dole queue. Work experience is one thing—this is altogether something else. It's a prison sentence for the crime of being young and jobless.

"Two secrets?" he heard himself repeating. I must get Maddy into the corridor. There's talking to be done. Yet John Spicer made no actual move to go. He felt a captive, partly to the image of the girl against the window, but now to this—yes, quite peculiar—situation. It held him as it seemed to hold Maddy.

Nothing of what John Spicer already knew fitted in to this place, these circumstances. Perhaps it was merely the light, its mysterious power of taking the substance out of things and turning them into shadows; perhaps it was the unfinished game of chess, its pieces representing promises which every move would disappoint; each player was a dream and an awakening. Mutually dependent, mutually destructive.

Mr Nelson's second secret was, "Where I stashed my money. My crock of gold."

John Spicer only nodded. Yes, old man, we know—somewhere over the rainbow.

"Our Maddy knows where I've stashed it, don't you, lass?"

Madeleine had moved her Queen's bishop. "I think it's check, Mr Nelson."

John Spicer suddenly felt, Maddy's not only working with the inmates, she's joined them. She wants the game to go on. Matron must have sensed this. If I don't do something, we'll lose the placement and placements in this town of the workless are gold dust.

Crocks of gold, in fact. Maddy must be transferred. We can keep her back in the Centre till her time runs out. She can do the staff lunches. That'll put an end to magic spellery. The Centre, with its schoolroom windows reaching to the roof and the smell of woodshavings from the craft shop, was no place for fantasies.

Of course, if Maddy's luminance were actually an inner light . . . but then it wasn't, was it? In the Centre she would always be what she was in her documents: seventeen, unqualified, unskilled and unemployed.

He felt strangely depressed about his decision. Madeleine of the Secrets: she touched his imagination as she had obviously stirred the imaginations of the residents of the Refuge of the Holy Saints Mary and Joseph.

"We can find another girl, Matron," he said as he was leaving. "I've not told Maddy anything yet, so if you could hang on with her till tomorrow, I'd be grateful. Allows me to sort out the paperwork."

"I'd rather she went straight away, Mr Spicer."

"That would look like the sack, and after all—"

"Very well—Friday." Matron considered John Spicer wet behind the ears. Sentimentalists shouldn't be running government training centres. His heart wasn't in his job, that was evident.

"Another day will allow Maddy to round off her case study."

"Case study!" thought Matron. "What nonsense."

Madeleine Rudge's case study had escaped check by cheating. He had accidentally on purpose knocked over his King and Queen and replaced them in each other's position. He stared at the deep-shadowed face opposite him. His was the grin of conspiracy. "Your gaffer thinks we was joking, lass. About the money."

Matron had not got all her own way with Mr Spicer; and she did not like the impression he seemed to have of her—that she was harsh. I have high standards, she told herself, but I am not unforgiving. Tension and irritation were in her voice when she returned to the room of the chess players. "Bath time, Mr Nelson. And no nonsense."

"Bath, Matron? I'm excused from bathing. Maddy here's going to get me a certificate."

"Maddy here is going to do nothing of the sort. Thursday is bathday even if you've got certificates to fill a jumbo jet. Of course as you claim to be the fastest man on earth, you may have the fastest bath on earth—but bath you must have."

"Me and this princess is going away together. We've booked passage for Hong Kong. The ship's waiting now."

"Ships don't sail to Hong Kong from this city any more. Now on with your flip-flops, Speedy Gonzales." Matron signalled for Maddy to stay where she was. "I'd like a word with you, Madeleine, if you please."

Mr Nelson protested that the chess game wasn't finished, that victory lay in his grasp. "Nobody will cheat, Mr Nelson. Nobody will move the pieces."

He was spiralling into a panic. It was not the game he was afraid of losing. He stared at Madeleine. "She's my friend, Matron."

"Of course she is, Mr Nelson. All of us—"

"Not all of you. Only Maddy . . . I've told her my secrets, haven't I, lass?"

Madeleine held the light enshrined around her. In the darkest aspect of her face—her eyes—there was a movement, which was enough.

"She cheers us up, Matron. Gives us hope, something to look forward to."

"Jaunts to Hong Kong?" Matron could not prevent a tone of contempt, even disgust, entering her voice.

"Just Maddy talking to us, that's all."

Mr Nelson took his turn to be silent, and his silence was more devastating than any further comment he could have made. He got up, dug his toes into the flip-flops. He leaned over the chessboard and upended his King. "That's the finish, Maddy, love." His hand reached towards her, touched a curl of her hair. He knew. "Good luck, lass. And remember my crock of gold."

"They're my friends, they've got used to me!" protested Madeleine when she heard of the termination of her Placement.

"I'm afraid all our inmates are past friendship, my dear. Most of them cannot even remember their own names from one day to the next."

"Because nobody talks to 'em—"

"Child, we'd all like to do that—"

"Would you?"

"In the best of all possible worlds—"

"But would you?" Madeleine had come out of her frame of light. The tranquil contours of the madonna hardened into flexed elbow and pointing finger. She was angry, accusing, part of the real world again. But this was not the persona of the girl in the documents. Quiet as a mouse? Unassertive? Inarticulate?

She was welling up with words. "Everybody's just a number here. You're waiting for 'em to die off. So you treat 'em like they was dead. You let 'em eat and bath and shit and nothink else."

"How dare you say that? You know nothing. You come without a certificate to your name. You fill the men's heads with fairy tales."

"They have dreams too!" hurled back Madeleine.

"Of crocks of gold?"

"Yes!" cried Maddy, with more conviction than she had ever shown in anything. "Yes, crocks of gold—real ones."

Matron sighed. She had much to do, all of it more important than quarrelling with a slip of a girl who had begun to believe her own fairy tales. "My dear, you've a lot to learn."

For the first time in her placements, for the first time since she'd joined the Scheme from the dole, Maddy gave vent to her feelings about the people that ruled her life. "Adults know everythink, don't they? So whatever we say or do, we get put down."

Matron had been here before: she prided herself on her understanding of the young as well as the old. "Not put down, my dear—"

"I'm not 'your dear'. I'm being booted out. Just when things . . ." She broke off. No longer the Madonna of the Window, she snarled like an alley cat. "Grown-ups make me sick. You're so superior. Yet all you do is make a bloody mess of our lives."

Struggling to remain calm and in control, Matron answered, "I'm wondering what that comment would look like on your documents."

"Stuff my documents!"

"Mr Spicer—"

"And stuff Mr Spicer. Stuff the lot of you!"

Matron stormed out of the room. "This will get reported —every word of it." She did not want to see Madeleine on the premises again, or she would summon the police.

Madeleine was left alone with her anger. She was not coming back and this made her sad. She looked around the room, at Mr Nelson's armchair, its wings worn to a gentle polish, its hand-rests frayed and darkened by spilt drinks; at the upturned King among the chess pieces. She stared out of the window on to the gardens. Beyond the immediate housetops she could make out the steel cranes along the dock road.

Not much use for those, these days. Join the club.

Goodbye Speedy Gonzales. He was an old bore, Mr Nelson. They were all old bores, endlessly repeating themselves, often in exactly the same phrases, with the same look in their eyes, daring you not to believe them. Yet sometimes there was more: a curtain opening on people who had once been real, smartpants, dressed to the nines, partings in their hair, on the make, full of beans and hope. Some of them even had been loved—desired!

I'll miss you.

Maddy went out through the proud Victorian doorway for the last time. She went along the marbled corridor to the attendants' changing room. Each potted plant on the way, each aspidistra, each blooming begonia, each dratted date palm, each frigging fern which Maddy had faithfully watered—she tipped over, spilling trails of soil behind her.

That's soil on my documents.

Mr Nelson and me, we're in the same boat. Without oars. Not knowing if we're sailing up the river or down it. Drifting. And at the end there's one of them weirs.

She suddenly stopped at the corner of the first floor stairs. Everything stood still except her brain. She turned. Instead of descending to the exit past that horrible statue, Plonker Peabody, she headed for the second floor, taking two steps at a time.

"I've told you my secrets, haven't I, lass? . . . She knows where I've stashed my crock of gold." Come back in a fortnight and Speedy Gonzales won't remember you. "That's the finish, Maddy, love."

He told me his secrets.

Has everything got to be a fairy tale?

The upper corridor was deserted except for an old man stooped against a window, staring, as Maddy had done, over the empty river. He was talking to someone who wasn't there—or at least not in Matron's world.

She went on up to the attic floor. Here Victorian grandeur ceased. Marble had given way under foot to creaking floorboards patched with lino. A right turn and along. The cleaners had not been up here in weeks. There was little point, for this floor was kept for guests of the patients. As none of them ever seemed to have a visitor for twenty minutes, never mind an overnight stay, the rooms were used for storage.

This door, number twenty-seven, stuck hard, but Madeleine overcame its awkwardness with a shoulder and knee. She was going to prove something, whether any promise in this world had a grain of truth in it, even if it was a crazy-man's promise.

"Hong Kong, lass, we'll sail to Hong Kong."

Where the flying fishes play. She liked the way he had put that. And the sun comes up like thunder out of China across the bay. She grinned at her own words: "They'll not let you on the captain's table in your flip-flops, Mr Nelson."

Maddy entered a bedroom suite. Bigger than our house put together. It was carpetless. Spare beds had been shunted in. They were stacked with blankets and sheets imprisoned in polythene. Adjoining the suite was a bathroom illuminated by a roof window of pearly glass.

The bath was full of black dust and dead spiders. Its feet, in the shape of claws, were thickly powdered with rust. A dust-congealed mat lay over bare boards.

Maddy was out of breath, not with stair-climbing, but with tension and a strange fear.

You'd better not have been kidding, Speedy.

At one time the bath had been boxed in with plywood and painted gloss white. The lengthward wall had been removed long since but the round end of the bath remained neatly tucked into its plywood casing. Tiny spots of rust showed where the nails were.

"Under here."

Maddy wrenched at the plywood, tore it upwards, stretched it against the nails which fought back tenaciously. The wood bent and snapped. She stripped out the pieces, prising away the vertical support.

The floorboards were thick with mouse droppings. Maddy the Mouse—who said that? One of the lads at the Centre. The others had all laughed. Even Maddy, because it was true.

In the world of the Centre, that is.

She brushed away the droppings. Are you listening, lass? The end board nearest the wall. Feel down. Yes, Mr Nelson, I'm feeling down. And you'll have space for two fingers.

Two fingers? Is this a joke?

It'll not bite, lass. And I want you to have it. No use to me. They'll not be letting me out. What with my speed, they daren't take the risk, in case the Ruskies kidnap me for a secret weapon.

Daft, like granddad. "Mr Nothink." But his head full of the big time. Fingers right under and pull. The floorboard came up as easily and as naturally as Arthur's sword from the rock.

Feel under, pet.

Maddy had to thrust her shoulder against the rim of the bath. She felt for the skirting board. In this position, she could not get leverage. She backed out. Now she came at the hole from beneath the slope of the bath, her head jammed under the rim. She coughed with the rising dust. Droppings squashed under her palm.

There was something. In dry, crackling paper. She had hold of it but it caught between the joists. She angled the package the other way.

The parcel of yellowing newspaper lay before her, held

together with two elastic bands which broke open at her touch. She shifted her prize into a pale oblong of light. On the front page of the *Liverpool Echo* was a picture of England's winning goal in the World Cup.

"It's older than me . . ."

Inside the cover was more wrapping, a tattered dishcloth which in its turn enclosed a brown washbag with a broken zip.

"More bloody paper!"

She unwrapped the rest. "Jesus, Mr Nelson!" Arranged as neatly and as thickly as new packs of playing cards, were five, ten and twenty pound notes.

Take it, lass, all of it. You show 'em.

Maddy counted Mr Nelson's crock of gold. It came to three thousand pounds exactly. She spread the notes on the floor in front of her. She held up a twenty pound note to the light. She had never seen one before. The watermark looked convincing.

"All my life . . ."

"Yes, pet?"

"There's been nothink round the corner—to look forward to, I mean."

"Pray for the best but fear the worst, eh?"

"Praying don't work." She had directed a wise smile at her case study. "But dreamin's better."

She sat upright. The evening light was endeavouring to cast her once more in its spell. Yet Maddy's expression was anything but serene. "And as for you, Matron—in future, you call me Madam!"

Although John Spicer had made a special effort on behalf of Madeleine Rudge to find her a new placement, and succeeded with great difficulty in getting her a trial run at the St George's playschool, come Monday she did not turn up at the Centre.

Another black mark to go down in her documents to add to Matron's comments about Maddy's bad language and insolence. John Spicer felt personally let down. It had seemed so unlike the girl.

You can never tell with young people these days. "Absolutely, Matron. I suppose you can say one thing, they can be depended on to disappoint you."

"I've not been able to get a sensible word out of her Mr Nelson since Madeleine left. Over and over again, he keeps repeating the lines from that song:

> *"Where the flying fishes play . . . Er—"*

John Spicer completed Kipling's line for Matron:

> *"An' the dawn comes up like thunder outer*
> *China 'crost the Bay!"*

"Yes. Over and over and over again. Poor child."

Spicer was not clear whether Matron was referring to old Mr Nelson or Maddy Rudge. He replaced the phone. "I'll 'poor child' her when I get my hands on her." No more kids on the Scheme would be allowed into the Refuge of the Holy Saints Mary and Joseph. Matron had been adamant.

No more dreams, no more fantasies. Just the facts. Meanwhile, Maddy would face her First Warning. Indeed her conduct warranted a Second (and Final) Warning. It was in the Regulations.

Certainly, a very serious word with her.

When she turned up, that is.

Tom Bleeding Who?

Course in a place like this what else can you do but talk to yourself? You'd go crazy otherwise. Anyways, you get to thinking. In my view the trouble with this world is people. I mean without them where'd be the hassle, and likely the main hassle is us lot, the blokes. If it's wars, you can blame us. If it's violence, if it's gangbangs, if it's torture, knee-capping, if it's pick 'andles at thirty paces, if it's bullets through the gizzard look no further than the male of the species.

I ought to know, I've a manslorter on me hands. That's killing when you only half meant it.

Funny though how we're all born of women. I mean why couldn't women have done a bit more to stop us turning out the way we have? Into slobs? Course women haven't no option really, not if you think about it. They get poddled and then it's the blokes who does the deciding like who's to be up to her elbows in kids' nappies and that. It's the blokes as bring in the loot and even if it isn't it's them as has the muscles. It's muscle I reckon that writes the rules in this world.

Take a look around you. Right?

Yet me I had no dad to speak of. Just me and me mam, neither of us with no muscle, so what happened? It's not stopped me bonecrushing, being your number one tearaway.

Mind you the real trouble about trouble is them things is enjoyable. That's where your toe rag teachers get it all wrong, and coppers and judges and them asshole politicians parroting on, they all forget or never knew that it's fun, specially if you risked getting caught, like smoking in the bogs, lobbing your half brick, burning your foreign car, slashing tyres all down the street so they'd have something to grouse about come Sunday morning, and not the least stirring up your racials.

Just like wars. Where else can you get a real thrill these days except when you're blasting heads off of parking metres or your yids and Pakis and of course being shit scared and coming through. All you need is to come through one time by the skin of your molers and the feeling, well it's terrif. As your thick-headed football stars say, TREMENDOUS! Drug crazy, real high.

It's not like winning on the pools cause that's only luck, it's cause you've achieved something, passed your test with flying colours. You always remember your first time. Mine was when we sunk this boat load of foreign tourist erks on Vicky Park lake, not that we wanted this spuke who couldn't swim to pass on to the next world, but then everybody's luck runs out sometime and you could argue only fools go on water if they're so bleeding cloth-brained that they can't swim. But like I say it weren't malice but his bad luck.

Same as our teacher Sambo Sir, whose luck's not been too good lately either.

It really give me the vomits him correcting my grammar. Spelling, well, everybody gets that wrong, even Shakespeare who couldn't spell his name right twice running, but grammar—specially coming from this Black meatloaf from the land of Tarzan where they don't have no clothes never mind grammar—it were a plain insult.

You don't say We was, Hank (that's my name though me mam calls me Henry which is a right poofter's name if ever there was one). You say, We were.

Well I always say We was and me mam says We was and me granny used to say We was, so who's Sambo Sir to give me the jug in public in front of me mates as all say We was and then to cap it all he makes things worse when I complained and he says Hank, it's because you've promise.

What a bleeding insult.

And on my patch. I could have accepted the arrogant prick if all he'd got to show were his cricket bat or he could spread his great raking feet over the hop step and Jerusalem at the Crystal Pally but what I couldn't stomach was him strutting his brain box in all directions.

His knowledge.

He was a walking talking encyclopaedia. About us, the Brits, rabbiting on and on about our history like it was his property, about Faraday and George Stephenson and Gladstone and Jane Austill, and then out of the blue he asks one morning, Any of you geniuses ever heard of Tom Paine?

Tom bleeding who? Well naturally the whole class has got a pain, we knows who's a pain all right, and we shouts We heard of Tom Thumb and Tom Fool, and we all sort of locate our pains, which reminds me it gave me a chance with Dorothy Parkin's boobs at last, with a ruler, a poke under the arm. You got a pain, Dot?

Anyways as it were all still rankling with me on account of my bad grammar I says to Sambo Sir Who's Tom Paine as if we actually wanted to know, and Sambo he comes a real cropper, cause he lets slip You Brits, yes Us Brits knows damn all about, how did he put it?—about what matters.

Us Brits, he says, is pig ignorant.

So we never heard of Tom Paine, that don't make us pigs and somebody yells from the back We all knows Tommy Johnson and he can beat up ten Blacks with one hand and work himself off with the other. Laugh, you should have heard it. The noise is so great it brings Daft Dave the head miser to see what the rum puss is all about.

Another black mark—Black, get it?—against Sambo Sir, for not being able to control his class.

And serves him right, Tom Bleeding Paine.

Being as old Sambo Sir never got round to telling us, I goes over to the school library, first time I darkened its doors, fact is I had to wait till the mob has gone to the chippy before I can take me face in that direction.

I felt as bad as asking for rubber johnnies. I wants a book, miss. Teachers is all the same. You *want* a book, says Lydia Loveless, a stringy bitch with real brains in a grey suit and a stupid bow tie on her blouse, but she's flabbergasted at me with no brick in me hand, and spotting a trick of course.

Me, a book, and natch she tries the funny bit. We got no books on bomb making, Hank. Cheek. If I wants to know that I'd not be skenning in no book, would I?

Which book, Hank?

And equally natch before I can say I want a book on Tom Bleeding Paine she says What exactly do you plan doing with *a* book, Hank?

You Brits. That really narked me, him just down from the trees correcting my grammar and knowing more about my street, my patch, my town and my country than I does. So I tells him. It's *my* country you're slagging off. He don't wear that: *Our* country, Hank, he says. Oh? *You* Brits, but *our* country. That's rich. It's not your bloody country, I says. Oh yea, he comes back, and he has a passport to prove it. Which is more than I've got or me mam's got or me gran ever had for that matter.

Then why call us that, Us Brits?

And he comes back fierce like, smart as your grinning cat, Because you makes a virtue of your ignorance. That took some sinking in. Left me like I'd walked into the back of a reversing bus. Dot did that once but her boobs saved her and they charged her mam for the dent in the bus.

Joke!

You parade it, he says. Parade your ignorance. Appreciated the way he put that—parade. Walking up and down Brick Lane toffed up in nothing but ignorance, and what narked me most was Sambo Sir being dead right.

Any of the mob as knows anything at all apart from your football, your screwing and your grievous bodily harum keeps it strictly private. Otherwise it's giving in to slobs. I mean if they've got to ram the stuff down your throat from moron till night then I reckon they're only doing it for their own benefit not ours.

Like as happened to Tar Baby when his mam wants him to take pianer lessons and he actually says he would. Pianer lessons! Holy mackerel! It took weeks to shave that tar off him. And the pianer, there weren't a squeak you could get out of it.

When it's all over you get to thinking. Me, I felt sorry for the old joanna but like I often says it seemed an okay thing to do at the time.

Anyways I was on about Us Brits as know nothing. I says to Sambo Sir after he talks about us parading our ignorance, Just because we never heard of your Tom Paine? I leaves out the bleeding bit this time to head off a sermon on bad language.

Not my Tom Paine, he says, yours. The greatest Englishman. Now this comment put pianer lessons in the shade all right. Greatest Englishman—and we never heard of him.

A real sod I'm telling myself, and he says, Pearl of British History, Tom Paine. He watches us from his seven feet up in the air, six of his own and one for the platform they built to make teachers feel superior, and we white goons go wild like only on our insides, but real sore.

Christ I'd heard of Henry the Eighth and Lord Nelson, Wellington and his boots, Puss in Boots, Lord Snowdon, Jimmy Greaves, Charles Dickens, Benjamin Disrooli and Macbath (course he were a bleeding Scot—bleeding? Thanks Hank), but who this Tom Paine were and what he did to win his title of Mr Universe, I couldn't guess to save me braces.

Which meant old Sambo Sir was going to get his own special braces and not to hold up his pants.

The greatest Englishman, he says, rubbing our noses in it, and none of you morons either knows nor cares, am I right? Dead right, as usual, or almost dead right. What he'd not quite put his finger on was that we'd nothing in particular against this Tom Paine bloke but a lot in particular about being found out, and accused.

That we cared about. So come Friday night or was it Saturday we goes round to this youth club where Sambo Sir's a steward with his wife in Brent. Bloody wonderfuel bird, plus Sambo's brains. Gerry goes up the stairs like a missile let loose by accident. Amazing how banisters is never safe as they're supposed to be. It was like a film, everything starts sailing about in the air. We really gets warmed up cause the stairs is as big as Westminster Abba (joke), meaning there's one hell of a drop and practically as wide as the Grand Can Can (another joke).

You should've seen this mountain of fertiliser growing and growing; tables, chairs, your bar billiards, lamps, rugs, the lighting trailing wires all over the shop, in fact so high was this pile getting that you could reach the first floor without going up the stairs. A real laugh.

And all because of this Tom Paine.

Fact is, Sambo Sir spoils the fun by saying nothing. Just stands in the bottom doorway whiles all his stuff come down. I mean, everything. After the furniture comes the cupboards, doors, shelfs crashing, bloody good loudspeakers. Josh took the record player. Funny thing, he never could get the swine to work at home. Said it was cursed, so he brings it back.

That was later when a few of us offered a bit of a truce. We didn't actually help Sambo Sir and his bird tidy up but we didn't actually stop em. Josh was very decent, he made em a cup of tea. As I was saying you do things then you get to thinking and soon we starts dropping in, specially on cold nights. The mob could do with a warm once the pub money runs out, and there is these snacks and things and gallons of tea.

He didn't call the police, not that that impressed us. We'd have appreciated another Armageddon from the Yard. Armageddon, I've been using that word a lot lately, only at first I thought it was Alma Ged On, and there was nowheres in the dictionary I could find it till Lydia Loveless puts me right. She springs up behind me on those flat rubber eels, sort of scrabby dame but with nice hips swaying like a tart between them bookshelfs.

The trick was getting the goods out of the library. They'll not get me queuing up for a ticket and if you've no tickets Lydia goes bananas. Berserk's better, that's another word I found flicking through the dictionary. Berserk's what Gerry gets every Saturday night and Friday nights if he can afford it.

Weighing up the field I thought even with a dictionary and the history of Samboland up me jumper I'd not have much more up front than Dot Parkin, and happen Lydia has her head as usual stuck in her card index, so I am through clean as a whistle.

Well it gives me the shock of me life this book on Africa. I mean, round our neck of the jungle they're such a bunch of lazy grots, plaiting their locks, jambing to their deafening music, being right pillocks when birds are around—and talk of racist.

Us whites is innocent as snow in comparison. I was doing the bike with Irwin and this Black geezer comes up, chats like. Okay, why not? Wanted to rub it in about the cricket. We says nothing cause he was twice the size of a centurion tank. Then this Paki goes past with his wife and his granny and out comes the speal from this hero, Paki bastards, eh, he says. Real wogs.

You could have knocked me over with a goose feather, and I thinks What makes you so special you Black ponce, and he says They wants repatriating. *They* wants, I mean who's country is this in the first place?

Natch I had to get a load of bollocks from Irwin, once the centurion has rolled on down the street, as Irwin's joined the Onion Jack Brigade and he comes out with his usual about the master race—that's us—and I thinks great, where's the evidence, what we got that's so bloody wonderfuel? Brains, money, a big house in Kent?

Anyhow this book drives me wild, well at first, and then I gets dead interested. These Sambos have had a civilsashun about six times as long as us lot. Palaces, roads, sewers, running water, they had laws and they could build bridges and aquiducks and all in all they knew what they was on about when we were still lobbing lumps of flint at dinosaurs.

Reading that book leaves me feeling like, well, a blooming native. It's us I tells me mam, who's wingeing on about the Blacks all the time, about them taking us jobs (jobs? what bleeding jobs?), it's us I says who is the kaffirs. It's us who wants repatriating. And she tries clouting me, not understanding a word I am saying, shouting (clouting and shouting—I ought to be a poet) Don't you go forgetting you're British, and I shouts back what Sambo Sir was hinting that time, If you don't know Tom Paine you don't deserve to be British.

According to this book on Samboland we Brits got tired of throwing rocks at terry dactyls and got to throwing em at wogs like and snaffling their land. We snuffed out (snaffling and snuffling, they ought to make me the next poet lorry ate) their civilsashun.

What do you know about them things, you ignoramoose? says me mam.

I knows for a fact.

You knows nothing son but drinking, hanging about street corners and getting in trouble with the police.

That's what you think.

That's what I knows, son.

I've been reading, Mam, I reply quiet like. I thought this'd get a response but it never registers.

You been trespassing and criminal damaging, that's what I knows. Down the club.

You going to shop me, Mam?

You'll shop yourself sooner or later, son. Mothers often get things right but she wasn't seeing nothing either, too tied up with her job and getting shoved around from clocking in to clocking out, dirt scared she'll get the push, and when she's home from nights she's too exhausted to speak.

Course on earlies she's too pissed by teatime to know the difference.

She was once a beauty, my mam. Seen it in her pictures, and even now the blokes throw her an eye. She's so wore down, wore out, like them all—Irwin's mam, Josh's mam, while Gerry's mam isn't around no more. Spared by cancer, her old man said. Bright spark, Gerry's dad, him being an electrician (got it, spark?—well, forget it), but him saying *spared* like that as if all that pain weren't no worse than what most folks have to put up with these days, it were so bitter.

Anyways the one bloke I should have gone to about Africa being a bit more impressive than a black asshole full of tsetse flies was Sambo Sir, and things being the way they was (the way they *were*, Hank, who'll ever give you an office job if you talks like that? I don't want no office job, thank you very much and of course he says You don't want *an* office job because if you say I don't want *no* office job it actually means that you *do* want an office job), well the way things were going (congratulations, Hank), to be seen to be talking to Sambo Sir about anything other than telling him to take the next train to Swaziland and painting his car with WOGS GO HOME, as I say any conversation in public or private for that matter would put me in hawk with the mob.

Put me in hawk? Where did I pick that one up, probably from Daft Dave who's full of bullshit words, it means getting trapped in the talons of a hawk maybe, which sounds right if you're wanting to get yourself an office job. Natch getting an office job would put me in hawk with the mob as would joining the Chelsea Scum over the Shed or going out with a bird on mob night, which is every night practically, or help paint the Club after we'd gone berserk with spray cans from the attic to the cellar.

Course Sambo don't object to the spray cans. All he says is, Just keep it grammatical, Hank. Keep it grammatical. So for a lark or to put him in hawk I goes round the school spraying it with WE DON'T WANT *ANY* EDUCATION instead of WE DON'T WANT *NO* EDUCATION. Only it changed the meaning like we was wanting *some* education but not *any* education which if you think about it makes more sense.

When Daft Dave shoots me out for it he isn't pinking as usual and he actually takes off his dark shades and talks to me. At least he says you got it grammatical, Hank, and that seemed to make a whole lot of difference, though Gerry gets his niggers into a twist about it, What you changed the line for, Hank, *any* education and I says Because it's grammatical, Gerry.

Grammatical! He comes back like I'd questioned his ancestry, What bollocks you jabbering about and I replies Grammatical's what them as passed their Eleven-Plus could speak and what got them office jobs and free cars and secretaries to sit on their knees.

Gerry's so impressed he knocks me through that hole in the fence down Bethnel Green and I rockets straight into this private meeting of the White Mafia Brethren.

Oops, Christ, it's a red spy in their midst from sunny Moscow.

Well that was the start of the serious trouble and no mistake.

Now each to his own as my gran used to say, or that's what mam used to say me gran used to say because by the time I was old enough to remember gran had departed to the Halls of Guinness (as granddad used to say according to gran, well that is according to mam). Each to his own and these gents had never been my taste of the month.

I mean if you wants to duff up the Blacks don't dress it

like it was Christmas carols and your duty to God and the Queen, just get stuck in. But not these laugh-a-minutes. They drones on and on about blood and homeland and national purity, like we was all virgins with no spots.

They've got this idea that us Brits, yes Us Brits again, have been robbed. If they're that worried and so much in love with this green and pheasant land why'd they spend so much time polishing their Nazi boots and gazing up at Appy Adolph and getting their stupid missuses to knit swastickers on their thermal underwear?

I knew what speech it was because I'd heard it before and they was to make me hear it again, about how Us Brits lost our greatness once we got mixed up with the wogs, which weren't the way this book tells it, in fact it were just the opposite. Fact is, we got mixed up with *them*, marching down their bamboo terraced houses first off and grabbing their balls and helping us selves to their comestibles.

Another word I came across that I fancied—comestibles. A bit of a disappointment when I looked it up and found it meant something you eats. Now which prick would invent a word like comestibles when they could simply say food? I'll tell you, a prick like me, because comestibles sounds mysterious, like jewels, treasure, something buried in a hole at the bottom of a miser's garden.

Anyway the Front lads took exception to me arriving plumb in their meeting chin first and in two seconds flat they have me pinned to the ground and shouting Heil Hitler at the top of me voice and Fatherland for Ever just to get out from under.

How they recognises me from school I don't know unless it was one of them round at four o'clock dishing out leaflets. I must have stuck in his mind because I actually stopped to read one, which was the same time as I was reading how we whites was exapropriating Africa for all it was worth and we've been blaming them ever since.

If you see what I mean.

I think I must have said something about getting a few

facts right, like it was us who'd been last down from the trees. Yes I remember he damn nearly choked me and here he was, same hand around me adman's apple and same bristles in his nose, screaming obscenities.

We've got a job for you sonnyboy they says when they'd done me over and taken my last fifty pee for their collection. Great I thought, with fifty million people unemployed, people with degrees and testimonials, and there's me being offered a job without asking.

How much?

Don't be cheeky sonnyboy it's all voluntary. Big joke I thought, voluntary or you gets your teeth stoved in, that's how they got Irwin.

Depending what muscle you possess it's either your roughhouse spot where you sort out them with the lip as comes to political meetings, ejaculate them and give em a close to death in some back alley, or it's ratting, standing at your street corners with eyes skinned. Or finding out the addresses of victims prior to the usual petrol sandwich job.

Irwin's got a brick head and muscles like Atlantic cables, but me I'm your Rambo after ten weeks hunger strike and they nails me for the job of lookout. That's after they've tanked us both up on Courage (joke, for that stuff only gives you the runs, get it?) and stiffened us backs with a few warnings about what'd happen if we muffed the job.

So there's this big meeting in our school, to celebrate the day Appy Adolph took over Germany and started short back and sizing the Reds and the Gypos and the Children of Israel not to mention their dads and mams and probably their grans and granddads as well.

Which surprised me our school letting them have a meeting like that. Real amazed till I latched on they'd been canny and booked it under a false name. Proper smart and it fooled Daft Dave and the Council. Even me gran wouldn't have objected to a meeting of the Local Amenities

Improvement Society. I got their leaflet, it was so respectable you'd have fallen asleep reading it.

They was expecting trouble (*were* expecting trouble, Hank). Yes, Sambo Sir, trouble from your direction, like a few of the enemy (which is anybody out there who don't agree with the White Mafia) gets wind of this Local Amenities whatsit and intends doing some local amenity improvement theirselfs.

Like fouling up this meeting.

Sambo Sir's going to be there representing Africa on Thames in the Black corner and Daft Dave because he has made a right mess of things like he always does. In fact all the teachers is going to turn out and a load of parents, them as aren't as pure as the Local Amenities Improvement Society.

Well that puts me in two minds because teachers is aggro from start to finish and the Jackboot Jimmys they got a point. Schools don't belong to teachers and the big wigs and if you wants to use a school hall which was built on the Rates and you pays your Rates, well it's right isn't it specially if you're willing to pay the hire fee?

That's freedom, that's how I seen it and if you want to slag somebody off why not as everybody's slagging everybody else off most of the time? Mind you not having no GCSE's (kept getting Yellow Fever and scurvy when they tested us) I don't suppose my opinion counts in these matters.

I asks Irwin and Gerry like and they says What's the odds, Friday night there's nothing on 'cept the pub and we got no gravy so let's do it for a laugh and who knows we could sample some of the collection.

I'd have appreciated Sambo Sir's point of view, being as how he comes from an ancient civilsashun but the last thing in the world any of us would do and live to tell the tale is ask the goon his opinion. That'd be stretching things too far, it would show as how we cared and round these parts caring's worse than a dose of the pox.

Fact is, I did care, to know what'd happen one way or the other. Born curious I guess, so that's why I goes along. How'd you know it were bad for the school according to Daft Dave in Assembly if it were only guesswork? After all the lads would only be preaching to other shagbrains, preaching as they say to the contorted and what does that harum?

And as for aggro you'd not get much feasting out of a fiver cause the police is going to be there in their thousands on account of their overtime.

Queer thing was, the teacher mob got talking about purity like what the Front was dong. That amused me. They was not all exactly using the word but there was all this crap about a place of education like it being special and unsullied (unsullied, how about that? which happens to purity when you leave her alone. Can you hear me, Dot? When you sick yourself on Saturday night you're sullied according to Lydia Loveless's dictionary). Anyways they were looking on our school like it was an innocent maiden being ravished (another word I got a real soft spot for) by the demons of Christ knows what.

All us lot can see is leaking roofs, broken windows and new kids passing out with them disinfectant fumes. It got everybody taking sides, that's what I'm saying. The best thing is, what starts off with a load of boring old farts yammering on about how the Blacks pinched our jobs in McDonald's and the Chinkys nicked our fish and chips and the Pakis stuck curry in our toad in the hole is likely to end up the nearest thing to Armageddon in Hackney since last Christmas when a few comrades over Clapton crashed the annual school disco and screw-in.

So I tells myself get your ass along as the Yanks say and have some fun, otherwise what will you have to tell your own kids and grandkids in future? Everybody else lives in their memories so why shouldn't us too as we'll have buggerall to look back on after sixty years on the dole.

Yet I'm wishing no damage to Sambo Sir, though even

I admit being biased that he's in for it one way or the other, him refusing to keep quiet, like he goes talking to the papers and making speeches and going round with his Labour Party badges. Soon, knowing the Lefties in these parts (my mam think's they're as big a turds as the Tories though in my humble opinion that'd be impossible), as I says soon they'll have him going for MP, which of course he'd do wonderfuel having twice the brains of the present incumbent (just come across that one, it means a bloke in a job who does eff all for what he's paid for).

You'd never be able to accuse Sambo Sir of sitting on his laurels (as me gran told me mam, Don't let the lad sit on his laurels, silly cow how can you sit on something you ain't got?). *Haven't* got, Hank, says Sambo Sir. Every time you open your mouth, lad, you murder your birthright.

Birthright? I says.

Your language, Hank.

That decided it, what with Us Brits and us not knowing about this Tom Paine, the greatest Englishmen and then being told I murder my birthright every time I opens me gob, well, what would you do?

The idea of making our school hall a place Millwall perverts would feel at home in, like all shit and violence, come to have a strong appeal after that because I was hoping something would get sorted out for good. I mean if the police loves the Fronters half as much as the Fronters says they do well the mob will walk over the enemy one way and the flatfoots will trample them in the dust the other way.

Still it were disturbing to have the police guarding every entrance and heaving protesters like hot cow clap across the school yard. Even Daft Dave was only allowed in the corridor next his room whiles us, we lorded it inside with this prat of a speaker spraying saliver to the back of the hall.

Suddenly there's this dwarf with the placard who oughter know better than wag it under Irwin's brother's nose (he had it hidden under his coat, the placard that is, not Irwin's brother's nose). Anyways merely to disturb the air round Irwin's brother is worse than stepping on a lion's tail, so he lands on this squirt, God how he landed.

You could feel it through the floorboards, then out the back and dumped in the skevvi bin on top of half the chemistry lab that's been jacked in cause of last month's fire, which I had positively nothing to do with as I was doing me homework at the time (no, honest).

Course that started things off real nice. We'd had enough speeches. Irwin's brother leads the attack and that sort of inspires Irwin who sets off Gerry and Gerry sets off Josh and that's how world wars get started.

Evenshally nobody knows who started wars but once you've got the action nobody knows how to stop it, right? That were an orntray or an ors doovre (Miss Stirwell taught us that in Domestic Science—Stirwell, got it?—as well as perryteefs like) yet the real meat and potatoes was outside in the school yard, all boxed and ready to be massacred, with the old iron rails behind em and the cops protecting the windows and bogs and us of course being the offended party.

They'd nowheres to go but up. There must have been seventy of us and I had to confess I weren't backward in coming forward. It was like it must have been at Waterloo, the battle I mean. It were kill or be killed and it were a smashing feeling cause everything seemed so simple, with your mates thugging beside you and the bosses and the teachers and all the other wankers who tells you what to do all day getting a right load of wind up their sails and giving us mouth like you never heard, like Swine and Scum and Vermin.

So the cops they keeps their distance, minding the property and probably remembering their own days at school when they got punched up hill and down dial and thinking Good on ye lads, or something like that. Anyhow we gets a free ride.

Natch it's Sambo Sir in the thick of the action, him a foot taller than the rest, real back to nature I thought, this

Black Napoleon spouting language that oughter get him struck off the teacher's registrar.

Talk about murdering his birthright.

Of course it's Sambo Sir the mob makes a beeline for. Get the Black four-letter word beginning with a C somebody yells and there's this roar like a volcano interrupting and I'm in the middle of it and nothing I can do about it. Me I got no grouse with Sambo Sir and in the rush I'm thinking Sambo's actually been a real pal off and on, more on than off if I cares to count.

I wrenches away and tries a knees in on this drainpipe with glasses and CND all over his chest. He goes down so easy I reckon he dropped on purpose, playing dead.

Still I was only kidding myself cause I knows what were happening to Sambo Sir, which when you thinks about it is what you'd expect. They had a photo of him at HQ with a dart through his eyes. I was asking myself just when the police would step in and sort things out cause your general duffing up is one thing but I'm not into chainsaw massacres and Sambo is getting it real hard, down on the deck, feet going into his head and boots on his chest.

I could see his blood trickling out his nose, not trickling actually but spurting and they weren't stopping, no intention of stopping and still the cops is standing around twiddling their flies.

I was in stuck what to do, I mean what would anybody do, wanting to shut my eyes and pretend I was someplace else, telling myself scram while you can and then all of a sudden I remembers Sambo Sir's still not bloody told me about Tom Paine.

Here he is on the point of spilling his guts all over the school yard and he's not spilled the beans like on the Greatest Englishman who puts Us to shame.

So right against the rules I goes blotting my copybook (Daft Dave's phrase, Don't go blotting your copybook, Hank, with bad company). Teachers they talk a foreign language of their own, have you noticed?

As I say, blotting my copybook I zooms in on my pals, trying to shift em off, get in between them and Sambo, catching one in the kisser myself and this rib which the Doc says will heal itself and shouting me tonsils out till I'm the colour of radishes when at last comes the moment when they steps in, the boys from the Met, like it were an excuse-me dance.

By this time we was both too late. It was sickening what they done to Sambo Sir, a sight to make you fetch up your dinner. Never seen damage on a person like it.

Your jugs of blood, yes that's normal with a do of this sort but not a skull bend in that far, over the eye. Somebody must have been using iron knuckles. I stood there never moving while the lads scarpered fast. You'll see nothing as fast as Nazis when they're not thirty to one on. Fifty fifty and they're over the hill and far away before you can say Tom Paine.

Course me face they knew, the cops and all that, and my name. It don't seem to have dawned on nobody that I was trying to lay em off our Sambo. All the witnesses as seen me remembered me giving me ten pence worth to this CND bloke and puts two and two together—incidentally making me look a right hero to the mob.

They writes me all these letters, makes me an award, Young Bulldog of the Year, and me mug's splashed over the front page of their newspaper.

In cases like this who listens to kids, so they slams the book at me it being easier than going out to catch them as was guilty. Not that Sambo Sir knows anything, him being in a coma for five weeks, to be exact thirty-four days and eight hours. I wonder if he'd speak for me even if he could.

According to me mam's grapevine like I'm the talk of the town, though she's not happy. Funny, she don't believe me one jot more than the others, the teachers, not Daft Dave, not Sambo Sir's bird, not them other protesters, not the police and certain not the heavy mob. They thinks I was doing my duty to God and the Queen.

Even Dot Parkin's given me the cold tit.

I been allowed to write to Sambo Sir. At least he'll get my side of the story as soon as he opens an eye, once his brain clicks back into action if it ever does. A whole pile of letters as high as that mountain of furniture in his club, till his bird writes she don't want no more letters and they come back with it written on Not Known at This Address.

If Sambo Sir pulls through they'll have me for attempted manslorter. Either way I'm lined up for a big future, I got the mark of Cain. I read about that in the Bible they stuff in your bedside drawer, about how Cain killed his brother Abel, and how God put this mark on Cain so nobody'd harum him and nobody'd do him any good (*any* good, hear that, Sambo Sir?) cause he was cursed. Which is real depressing.

There's been plenty to read in this place and I got all these books to meself, Sambo Sir would be right pleased. I'd like him to know well all this business about taking sides, looking back it's not how I'd want it but there's been no way to get it sorted.

Now it's probably too late.

The big news Sambo Sir is that I've found it, I come across old Tom Paine, unbelievable in a dump like this. His book has the price on the front, predecimalshun like, five shillings. That's twenty-five pence and I've been through his ideas from start to finish, then over again.

You got it spot on Sambo Sir. Him as can write about important things like that deserves a statue bigger than Nelson and Wellington put together. Anyhow that's my opinion.

Well that's the bell for lights out. I am praying for your brain to be stuck back in good order, Sambo Sir. And thanks. Folks should read Tom Paine. Yes, he's the greatest of Us Brits, no question. His book's called *The Rights of Man*. It's about how the world's a struggle between Reason and Ignorance.

Reason and Ignorance. I'd go along with that.

This Nothing Will Never End

Freely adapted from 'The Well' by Augusto Cespedes, an account in diary-form of events which took place during the Chaco War between Bolivia and Paraguay, 1932–35. Cespedes was born in Cochabamba, Bolivia, 1904. Now in his eighties, Cespedes is Bolivian ambassador to UNESCO in Paris.

The English version of his story was published in *The Green Continent: A Comprehensive View of Latin America By Its Leading Writers*, selected and edited by Germán Arciniegas (US: Alfred A. Knopf, 1954). This adaptation is dedicated to Cespedes and to the many Latin American writers who have given me such pleasure over the years.

Already used to daily blindness, he was choking on dust. You never get used to the dust. He stumbled over the handle of his pick. He crouched coughing over the black earth. He heard the bugle-call from above, yet the force of the earth had sucked out the last of his strength.

"Carlos!"

It was his time. He brushed mosquitoes from his bare legs. He heard the bugle summons once more and again his name being called; so far away, up and up in a patch of white sky as distant as the stars.

He had been on the sick-list. Sarge had spared him from the digging—for two days, but he had not wanted to be counted a shirker. Too early back, dizzy on the journey into the dry pit, down on the leather belt, the singing rope, down into such depths as changed a person; rendered him part of the earth, with its smells and its towering walls and its crushing darkness.

Made him like a creature born to burrow for a lifetime in mud and through mud to desert and through desert to mud again.

Yet never water.

Never what they were all searching for. Never that. "This nothing will never end," Sergeant Najaya had said. An educated man, the Sarge. Yet he too, despite all his book-learning—what was he? No better than a mole, sweating away the seconds of his life with paws not hands, with appendages that tore at the soil, hurled at the soil as if to work frantically would somehow conquer time, make it move faster.

It never did. Down here time was at a standstill. Down here in the darkness of the well time had no meaning. Only the bugle-call meant anything and now Carlos did not answer.

He was being tugged towards earth. He did not resist for in his fading there was light, a twist of it beyond his hands, a snake of light, uncoiling, gliding, of a silver colour, glowing.

Carlos fell back on his haunches. He was witnessing Cosni's dream; old Cosni who wasn't that old, but battles had scarred him. The heat of the Chaco had robbed Cosni of his middle age as it had begun to rob Carlos of his youth. There was scarcely enough flesh on Cosni to stretch over his bones.

"I dreamt," said Cosni, as the men lay in the cool of the evening beside the earth-mounds from the well, "of this silver serpent. It was made of pure water. It sparkled yet stayed exactly in the serpent's shape, and in the well it slid towards me. I felt it go round me, cool and fresh. I dipped my hand into its skin and as I did so the serpent began to grow larger. It rose up the pit with me riding on its noble forehead like a king."

Cosni continued, "When we reached the top of the shaft, everything about me had changed. The desert was gone. All these parched trees, with more branches than leaves, they were a green forest, so thick not a beam of sunlight could pierce the shade.

"Beyond the forest, the desert scrub had become green fields, fields full of corn, and everywhere there were streams. You could see the fish jumping. It was a new world, comrades! Yet—" and here Cosni had stumbled into sadness, bowed in the faint crimson of the watchfire, his face still dust covered, dust in his eyelashes, dust in the creases of his skin, "Yet however much of the water I drank, my thirst was never quenched. Never!"

This nothing, will it never end?

When Carlos did not answer the bugle-call two of the sappers came down for him: sturdy Pedraza with his tales of the war, for he had been in it from the start, "And I still don't know what it's about, Comrades!" and Irusta from La Paz with his jutting cheekbones and slanting eyes that made him look more mournful than he really was.

Chacon from Potosi stared over the lip of the pit and shouted, "Is he all right?" His voice carried no further than the first month's digging. At this depth, at fifty odd metres and still not a gleam of dampness, only the bugle had the carrying power to be heard.

Carlos was hoisted up on the pulley, dangling loose, half awake, half in Cosni's dream. "Kids like him," said Pedraza, "should only do half a shift."

"I'm not a kid." Carlos' eyes were open, burning. He threw off the harness that had held him.

"True," affirmed Cosni, "he's not a kid. Look, he's up to here"—he placed the flat of his hand against the bridge of his nose, laughing, "and still growing."

Chacon shook his head. "That well will stunt his growth."

"Not if we find water," said Pedraza. "Then you'll see how he'll shoot up."

Carlos lay under his blanket, shivering. After the desert heat of the day, this night air was also of the earth, clammy, penetrating skin and fat till it chilled the heart.

There was never ever silence. The hours of light were ruled by the drilling monotones of locusts. The only competition came from bees, tiny creatures hardly bigger than flies. Heaven knew where they came from, yet at every hint of water, they swarmed. If you wet your hair they tangled in it and you had to fight them off. Luckily they were too small or too weak or perhaps too wise to sting you.

And of course there was the gunfire from the battlefront —wherever that was. It kept shifting, sometimes close, sometimes far off. But it was never relevant to the diggers of the well, except that if there had been no war there would have been no thirsty soldiers; and there would have been no need to dig a well.

One small miracle occurred each time the provisions truck arrived with stores and precious water: out came the butterflies from the skeleton shade of trees and shrub. Where the water ration was poured into cans, the butterflies flitted close enough to the ground to make shadows, alighting on each spot of water-discoloured sand.

"Like little hearts," Pedraza had described them. "They're the spirits of our women back home, eh, come to visit us?"

By night the animals found their voices. From among the stunted trees, from across the milk-white moon-still Chaco, came shrieks and howls and cries like the wailing of children.

"You'd think the animals would be used to the dark," considering Sergeant Najaya, "and yet they seem to have worse nightmares than we do. This is a haunted land, and utterly worthless."

Carlos too gave voice to his terror of the night. It made him ashamed for it was in his sleep that he cried out; and in his shame he would fight against sleep.

"Sometimes, lad," Chacon had once said to him, "you're like all the night animals rolled into one."

"Then will you wake me, not let me go on?"

None of the sappers would oblige him. "You need your sleep, lad," Chacon answered. "It doesn't bother us if you scream your head off."

"It's The Thing," Irusta ventured to explain; the hole was always addressed as The Thing because it seemed more alive than the diggers. "It's got into all of us. It's a spirit."

Cosni had grinned, revealing chewed tobacco in wet teeth, "We're digging into a god's behind, and he's put the lot of us under a curse."

"We'll find water," insisted Pedraza, who had first drawn attention to the hole. It had not made him popular. Before The Thing had filled the sappers' lives, they had built roads. That was bad enough, for they always turned out to be roads to nowhere.

Roads to the Front, and then suddenly the Front would move and the roads were abandoned. Only armies needed roads in this desert land.

"Listen," Sarge had said with a view to restoring the morale of the men, "what's the difference between building a road that goes nowhere and digging a water hole with no water?"

"You tell us, Sarge."

Sergeant Najaya, whom the men sometimes called The Philosopher, had paused for thought. He decided against trying to kid his men. He had smiled. "If anybody's got an answer to that, I'd appreciate it if he'd let me know."

When Carlos had first joined the troop he had not considered himself old enough to ask the question, Why are we fighting? His question had been, Who are we fighting?

Eyes bright with fever, gleaming in the dark, eyes refusing to close despite his infinite tiredness, he remembered Cosni, ever-cynical, answer:

"We are fighting our brothers in suffering, who else?"

Chacon misunderstood. "The Pilas are no brothers of mine." He shifted awkwardly on the bone-hard earth. "Though I've a cousin who married a Paraguayan girl. They make good wives."

Pedraza asked, "Where are you from, Carlos, that you know so little?"

"The village."

"You mean *a* village—which village, son?"

"My village."

"What's its name, if it still exists?"

"My village—I don't know what its name was."

"The lad's an imbecile."

"Why did you leave?"

"Nobody to stay for. All dead." It was always in this manner that the autobiography of Carlos closed, in awkward silence.

Cosni had summed it up long ago: "The boy's come from dust. He joins us in dust and that's where we'll all end—dust."

Which had caused a row. Chacon blamed Pedraza. "You got us into this choking mess, with your bright ideas about digging wells. You've condemned us all to dust."

"We'll find water!" insisted Pedraza. He strove for conviction: "We've got to find water. We deserve it!"

Everybody laughed. Deserving something—that was a joke as cruel as the Chaco.

Pedraza was not to blame. Carlos admired him because he never surrendered to hopelessness, and he had only been trying to help once the bad news reached camp.

First, the water truck failed to make its daily appointment. The men had waited and watched on the earth mountains, ebony figures against the scarlet of fading day. No truck came.

The tortures began. The truck was their clock of life. Without it, everything collapsed, body and spirit. Tongues burnt beyond endurance. With the sulphur heat of morning, skin already covered in scabs became bleached, prickling, unbearable to the touch.

When the truck did appear a day late, the men were down the road waving and cheering as if there had been a declaration of peace.

The truck driver's announcement turned cheers to wails of protest. "The creek's all dried up." He eased himself from the oven of his cab, wiping sweat from his brow with a dirty arm, leaving dirt on dirt. "That means the regiment's desperate. In future water'll have to come up from La China."

"Are you crazy?—that far?"

"They've ordered reduced rations."

"Reduced? The man *is* crazy. What we supposed to live on, fresh air?"

"They say the Pilas are worse off than us." The driver scratched his red neck, leaving black knuckle marks. "I'm sorry, it'll be two days before I'm back."

Cosni said, "You can spend weeks dying of hunger, but you can die of thirst overnight."

It was then Pedraza suggested the old well-dig three kilometres away, begun and then abandoned by the Pilas; a hole overgrown now with bushes, its only landmark a palobobo tree. "It's worth a try."

Sergeant Najaya had thought so too: "Better than building roads to nowhere."

As if in anticipation of these words, orders came from headquarters: cease digging roads. Water is at a premium. Dig wells.

And The Thing had come immediately to life. It was a dragon, a fiery furnace, a monster from outer space. Its appetite was insatiable. As the sappers created the void, the void consumed them. As they created darkness it swallowed them, daily a little more of themselves, their hopes, their life force.

All of them except Carlos, that is. For him, as with the others, The Thing had come to dwell within him. Yet for him it was something to wonder at; as it grew deeper and deeper, something to marvel at.

To the men, the old lags, dreams of being carried up from the depths on a spout of crystalline water were fantasies of the night. They were not signs of faith but of despair. To Carlos in his simplicity they were visions of what might be. They were the stories of his snatched-away childhood. The pit was where present and past and future fused in his imagination.

Carlos, always of few words, kept such visions to himself. He would nurse his thoughts. As though stealing glances at a forbidden photograph, he recalled the abiding image of his past—the grand tunnel which had been to him both to terror and a joy.

In Carlos' village, the one without a name, the tunnel had belonged to the children of every generation. It was the secret nobody kept and as each generation grew to parenthood it forgot the joys the tunnel gave and remembered only its terrors.

Don't go near the tunnel, children.

Don't go near the tunnel or the monster-man will get you, Old Nick will carry you off to his roasting-pot.

It cut clean and steep into the hill outside the village; a sacred hill, so people claimed, where the Indian folk buried their dead before they had been driven off the land by white settlers.

Haunted ground, cursed ground.

Don't go near the tunnel, children. There is bad air, poisoned air. There are quicksands in its centre that have sucked many a disobedient wretch to its death. There are ravens in the dark waiting to swoop down and peck out your eyes.

With such warnings jangling in their ears, each generation of the village children chose the path of disobedience. They thrived on the poisoned air. To protect themselves against Old Nick they carried crossed twigs tied with hemp. As defence against frenzied ravens they fashioned cardboard visors. In case of quicksands, they carried slats from fruit boxes.

And eventually they took nothing with them but their hands and knees; which is not to say that they grew unafraid. The tunnel did not need Old Nick, ravens or quicksands to strike terror into each heart. Darkness did that for them, and narrowness, and the closing in, and the need to crouch and then wriggle behind the precious candle-end.

For Carlos, his trepidation concealed by a face of bravado —at least while the other kids were watching—there always came second thoughts. His mother had been a wise woman, with sense enough only to make a fuss over things that really mattered. She pleaded with him not to enter the tunnel.

"Sometimes the roof caves in," she said. "There can be no worse death than suffocating in the darkness."

Carlos knew that there were worse deaths. His mother had proved this to him: she had died a worse death.

Second thoughts stirred up the imagination. He pictured gruesome disasters, of being attacked by giant spiders that eat you while you are still alive, of being smothered by rats in their hundreds, of stumbling into a nest of poisonous snakes.

They were never enough to deter him from the journey; indeed the worse the horrors, the more he felt compelled to beat them. Then, as the centre of the tunnel was reached—terror, indescribable, welling up in the silence, when going back was pointless and where the real monster was oneself.

"I am Carlos." On his first journey alone, he had spoken the words aloud. "I am Carlos." That is all, but it seemed sufficient to drive him on until finally and burstingly there was joy—the gleam of white sky at the tunnel's end.

It was the moment of paradise: far off still, but reachable and as magnificent as the great fountain which bore Cosni to his vision of a land flowing with milk and honey.

Terror and joy; as for The Thing, it had given the diggers much terror and no joy. For all their labours, they only glimpsed paradise when they were in retreat.

Weeks ago they had suddenly struck mud. The men had cheered and danced as though they had discovered gold, not dampness. They had rested up for a few days to see if the water would seep out of the mud and fill the hole.

Pedraza's good humour returned. "Sarge, how about inviting the General to come and cool his ass in our pool?"

The mud oozed nothing but breathlessness. The earth became dry again. Hard dirt.

April, thirty-five metres deep, and nothing. The men protested. "It's hopeless," said Chacon. Sergeant Najaya duly reported the bad news to command. A captain came out to inspect.

"We must have water."

"There's no water. We must try somewhere else."

The captain had looked into the bottomless dark. He was a mathematician of a sort. "Two wells thirty-five metres deep won't give us water." His slow thoughts interrogated the earth. "But one well seventy metres deep—that might find us water."

"Yes Captain."

"You may be within days, or even hours of striking water. Think of the celebrations!"

"Celebrations, yes, Captain."

"All right, then let us show faith. Another little effort. We must, for the men are dying of thirst."

Only the promise of increased rations of coca and water made the sappers return to work.

"But if it's hopeless, Sarge?" asked Irusta.

"We press on. This is war, after all."

Only Carlos celebrated, felt the load slip from his heart, for he believed—yes, there would be water. Its discovery would give him the same joy that the end of the tunnel had given him. He took the first turn down the well, for there were no other volunteers.

"Each shift," ordered Sergeant Najaya, "will be reduced from an hour to three-quarters."

Carlos was winched from view, his mind empty of everything but the past. Yet his senses were all of the present—eyes shut off from sight except for the dim shape of hands on the pick, black on black, as soil revealed soil; ears catching only the desperate lunge after breath, for down here air evaporated like water on sun-scalding stones.

Here truly was the future: the black tomb, the earth in which Carlos and the others would rot; here was the smell of it.

Sergeant Najaya had promised, "Death'll be no surprise."

Cosni's dream, of the serpent of endless water, lodged

in the heads of the diggers. Even stern Irusta, made of earth and rock, his face a crag with hollowed eyes, began to prophesy success. "My pick struck chunks of solid ice," he claimed, while Chacon declared he had touched off the ripples of a subterranean lake.

"There's a light down there. I saw it. Glorious!"

Carlos alone did not dream, had no visions. Only he seemed content to dig with a pick that was not a magic wand in a dry hole that was not an enchanted well.

He could not explain this. The others wondered at his dreamless devotion, but they could not explain it either.

"Perhaps you have a dream like the rest of us," suggested Pedraza, "but it slips away before morning."

"Perhaps," said Carlos. He thought, there would be nothing like the real thing, the water gushing up into his arms, enfolding him, cascading over his face and hair, turning this horrible throat from desert to green plain, from the abomination of the Chaco to the sweet fields of his homeland.

Perhaps.

Also, it had to be admitted, down here there were no bullets. Whatever evil lurked in the heart of The Thing, it was not man-made. It did not scream out of the sky and blow the innocent and the unsuspecting into a hundred pieces.

"This lad," decided Cosni, "doesn't want to find water. Fact is, he'd be disappointed. Am I right, young Carlos?"

The boy answered only to himself: if we do not find water they will make us go on digging, and if we go on digging the war may end.

What mattered most to Carlos was that the war would forget him. Destiny had other plans.

There had been the Colonel's visit. Orders cast down the well had not been heard; sappers went on working, deaf to the world of sky and light, alive only to dust and mosquitos, to the throbbing of swollen hands and feet.

So the Colonel sent packs of cigarettes and a bugle. First it had been Pedraza who did not respond to the bugle-call.

His body had been dragged up and lay motionless for a while in the poor shade of the palobobo tree. Then Chacon fainted and eventually came Carlos' turn.

The diggers knew how dry The Thing was. It was no well, never would be. "We'll reach hellfire first," Cosni had said, and the camp agreed. It was time to admit defeat.

At this same moment a strange whisper had gone out from the head of the shaft, a rumour whose power multiplied at every telling, of a well which had reached such a profound depth that surely there was water, or why would the sappers go on digging?

The story spread through the Bolivian ranks at the battlefront.

You heard of this well?

Aye, deeper than any on the Chaco.

The officers say it's dry.

They would, wouldn't they? Military secrets, like.

So as to fool the enemy.

Right.

There's an underground lake.

Fountains, I've heard.

Once the war's over, they're going to settle that desert. Irrigate the land.

And if the Pilas find out, what then?

The driver of the provisions truck carried home the rumours. "You're famous, lads—heroes! This hole in the ground's got the brigade talking more than Ruby Keeler's legs!"

To begin with, the sappers reacted with numb incomprehension. Then they began to wonder—had the Colonel some knowledge, gleaned perhaps from a geologist, that there really were underground streams; was that why he had been so perky, so generous with his fags—did he *know*?

The rumours were so pervasive, so free of doubt, that the men took heart. They dug with a relish they had never shown before. The Thing was no longer addressed with contempt; rather it became "our well". What had been no well now became *the* well.

As all rumours must in time of war, the stories crossed into the enemy lines where thirst was also an abomination, where supplying the troops with water required ever-longer journeys and where water was the heart of every fantasy and every dream.

The Bolivars have struck water. The well is so deep it opens into a crystal lake hundreds of metres wide.

Every day squads are sent up to bathe in it.

They're going to irrigate the desert with it.

That well could win them the war.

On the first day of October, the order came to stop digging. Seven months and not one drop of water; no sign of it, now or ever. Those were the facts.

It had become a daily ritual for Sergeant Najaya to greet each man arising from the tomb of dust and darkness, black with sweat, with the words, "How about it?"

"Just the same, Sarge, nothing."

And Najaya, an educated man, loathing his position but most times bravely silent, would reply, "Always nothing, just like the war. This nothing will never end."

That is not how the Paraguayans had come to perceive the situation. They had learnt of the well from a captured enemy soldier. He told them all he had heard. Of course, he said, it was only gossip, of a magnificent well beside a palobobo tree.

At dawn on the fourth day of October Carlos awoke to hear rifle fire. He had lived with such sounds, off and on, for months, but the guns had always been distant, muffled; they were the bullets of another war in another place.

Sergeant Najaya's voice was cockcrow. "Rifles!" The Paraguayan troops had advanced in darkness to within four hundred metres of the encampment.

Carlos yanked himself up, sick with fear. There was momentary panic among the half-awake sappers till Najaya brought them to order, flat on earth mounds, the sun beginning to scorch them with its traitorous light.

The rifle fire of the Pilas was only the overture to this tragi-comic opera of the Chaco War. Carlos rammed his head into earth as machine gun fire raked the camp, crackling in the barren copses of trees.

"The forward trenches—they've been taken!"

"Christ, that means—"

Two Stokes grenades fell behind the sappers' tents, unearthing them and everything the men possessed. Pedraza chose to laugh. "They've heard of our lovely water!"

Chacon growled, "Crept up on us like cowards. And it's our water they want, God curse them. We dig, they drink, is that it?"

Our water.

Carlos heard the words: our water. Chin on earth, cheek jammed against the butt of a dirty rifle, he sensed a force within him:

Our water.

Irusta, veteran of other battles, at Yujra and Cabo Castillo, said, "Let's give 'em hell, make them earn their drink."

Though the unit were merely sappers, trained in the combat of picks and shovels, they fought with great bravery. They fought with a belief which even Cosni, the cynic, did not challenge.

An officer came down between the earth mountains with a squad of soldiers and a machine gun. He was curiously unwelcome. "Orders," he yelled, "to defend the well at any cost."

Defend the well: orders from the very top of army command.

Defend the well.

At any cost.

This command from an outsider, an interloper, angered the sappers.

Defend the well at any cost.

Isn't that what we are doing?

"A well with no water?" grimaced Cosni. "He orders us to defend a well with no water at any cost?"

The men went on fighting with courage, but their faith—their vision of water—left them. The enemy could be forgiven their desperate assault on the well because only by capturing it would they prove once and for all whether it contained water.

To be ordered by one's own side to defend a waterless well at any cost was beyond forgiveness.

Carlos struggled to understand, even amid the gunfire he wanted to understand.

Could Pedraza explain it? "Okay, we've no water," he said. "But the Pilas don't know that."

There was silence, gun-deafening but word-silent, until Sergeant Najaya put all matters into perspective. "Of all the animals in the living world," he said, "man has got to be the most stupid."

The Chaco War suddenly concentrated its ferocity on this patch of dry earth, this circle of dust mounds at the centre of which was a hole of meaningless depth.

For this men died. Cannon fire split skulls as the trunk of the palobobo tree had been split. The sappers irrigated the dust with their blood. From this feast the thirsting butterflies were to stay away, leaving the mosquitos to gorge themselves.

Carlos' finger closed on his rifle trigger. The bullet screamed at the sun. He took ages reloading and in this time Cosni died with bullets through his shoulder and across his jaw. Beside him too lay Irusta, face up at the vacant sky, no wounds evident. Perhaps it was his slant eyes at this angle which, in death, made him appear as if he were grinning.

Sergeant Najaya had reached over and closed Irusta's eyes for ever.

Chacon was hit towards midday, his body carried with the impact of the bullets almost to the edge of the well.

Pedraza, whose well this had become more dearly than the others, fought as though beneath him, huddled in his loins, were his only child. He fought as a tiger, fought for dead earth, for an empty space.

In his dying he shielded Carlos from the full blast of the Pilas' attack.

By the time the sun reached the high furnace of the day, Carlos' arm hung shattered and useless. His eyes stared into death. His companions were gone. Only Sergeant Najaya, wounded but not seriously enough to prevent his fighting on, remained of those who had dug the well; who had created The Thing.

"We did it!" Najaya referred to the withdrawal of the enemy, leaving, on their side, many dead. They too had fought like tigers. They had almost, but not quite, achieved their miraculous goal—the capture of a well without water.

"Help me," said the Sarge as the ceasefire stretched on into the afternoon. It was clear that the Paraguayan troops had been ordered back to their lines. "Give us a hand, son."

Carlos nodded. He had been bandaged up. For the moment he could cope with the pain. He would never pull trigger again, nor dig for that matter.

"Into the well," ordered Najaya. "It's what they'd have wanted. After all, why dig new graves?"

Carlos understood. In war you dig your own grave; the well meant that much.

Together he and the Sergeant dragged the sappers to the edge of the great void. Najaya tipped them over one by one, whispering a hurried prayer—for Chacon, Cosni, Irusta, for poor Pedraza, for the Indians who had died as mutely as they had lived.

Over the lip of earth and lightlessly into nothing. This private ceremony over, Sarge called other labour to shovel earth over the far-deep graves while Carlos stood in the sun. He was glad that sweat and dirt camouflaged his tears; but then weeping became all right when Sarge spilled tears of his own.

Carlos appreciated that. For once, the well had sprung true water. He wept aloud and in his head the crystal fountain rose up till it trembled against the cloudless sky.

Smiley

"Squa-a-a-d shun! A-a-t ease. Again, squa-a-ad shun. A-a-t ease. Squa-a-a-d shun. You boy?"
"Sir?"
"Don't address me as Sir."
"No Sir."
"Bombardier to you."
"Yes Sir!"
"Bombardier!"
"Bombardier Sir!"
"Boy, are you funning me?"
"Me, Sir?"
"Bombardier."
"Yes—"
"So you are?"
"No Sir!"
"No Bombardier!"
"No Bombardier."
"Then why are you grinning?"
"I'm not Sir."
"You're not *Bombardier*."
"I'm not Bombardier."
"Not what, boy?"
"I forgot Sir."
"If you're funning me, soldier."
"I'm not er, funning you, Bombardier."
"Then tell me why you are grinning."
"I'm not."
"You're grinning, boy. You've been grinning ever since you joined this parade."
"No Sir."

"No *Bombardier*."

"Not grinning, Bombardier."

"You are calling me a liar?"

"No Bombardier."

"Then you admit you are grinning."

"No Bombardier."

"I am a liar then. I look at you. I see that you are grinning like the Cheshire cat from ear to ear and you say you are not grinning."

"It's my face, Sir."

"Bombardier."

"I can't help it, Bombardier."

"Help what?"

"My face."

"You are funning me, soldier!"

"No Sir!"

"No Bombardier! Step forward, boy . . . Lance Bombardier?"

"Yes Bombardier?"

"Your opinion. Look into this soldier's face, if you please."

"Bombardier?"

"And tell me whether in your view he is grinning . . . Well?"

"He's grinning, Bombardier."

"From ear to ear?"

"From ear to ear, Bombardier."

"That makes two of us liars."

"It's my face, Bombardier. I can't help it. Honest."

"We have finished speaking to you, boy . . . Lance Bombardier?"

"Bombardier?"

"What do we do with squaddies who call their betters and superiors liars?"

"We wipe the grin off their faces, Bombardier."

"Then we have no option in this case."

"No option, Bombardier."

"Squa-a-a-d, at ease! Not you, soldier. A-tten-shun! Now I am going to give you one chance, and one chance only, to remove that grin."

"It's not a grin, Bombardier."

"You refuse?"

"But Sir—"

"*Bombardier!*"

"But Bombardier—"

"March him, Lance Bombardier. To the bottom of the parade ground, then two circuits at the double."

"But Bombardier—"

"March him. Then at the double. Full pack."

"Have we cured you, soldier? Boy, do you hear me? Straighten up. Have we cured you?"

"Bombardier, I'm—"

"Shagged out? Not a bit of it. We've all day to get things right. Well Lance Bombardier, is he still smiling? Look hard."

"He says it's the way his face is made, Bombardier. They all call him Smiley."

"Is the boy grinning, Lance Bombardier?"

"Well—"

"Grinning!"

"It looks—"

"In my view he is still grinning. Funning me, funning you, funning the regiment."

"No Sir!"

"*Bombardier*! You see?—funning us. Then we shall wipe the grin off his face. The squad is watching, Lance Bombardier. It is a trial of strength, as they say . . . Wipe that grin off your face, boy."

"Can't Bombardier. It's my face. They all call me Smiley —don't you?"

"Do not look round, soldier. You are alone here. These soldiers are statues. They do not smile, they do not grin and they do not speak. Atten-shun! At ease! They do what

I tell them, exactly and to the split second. I am telling you to wipe the grin off your face."

"I'm doing my best, Bombardier."

"He's trying, Bombardier."

"He's trying my patience—see! Ear to ear. You're an insolent little rat—what are you?"

"An insolent little rat."

"So wipe off that grin!"

"I can't Sir!"

"Can't? Won't! You are making a monkey of us, all of us."

"Can't."

"Lance Bombardier? Four circuits at the double."

"Four?"

"Four! We'll wipe the grin off that face, Christ Almighty we will. At the double, remember."

"Pick him up, Lance Bombardier."

"He's done, Bombardier."

"Pick him up . . . You two, hold this boy erect."

"He's promised, Bombardier."

"Promised?"

"Not to grin. Not smile. He's a point, it's his face."

"I can't see his face."

"Sweat, Bombardier."

"Hold his head up. You boy, hold it, tilt it—under the chin. So?"

"Bombardier?"

"Have we made progress? I think not. You are still smiling, boy. Half dead and still smiling . . . What does he say?"

"He says No, Bombardier. It's his face."

"I am of the opinion that it is more than that."

"More?"

"It is what lies behind the face which is the problem. What is in his head. His insolence."

"No Bombardier—"

"Yes Lance Bombardier. Obviously you do not see it. Hold the face. Am I right, he is still grinning at us."

"It's a joke in the billet, Bombardier. The shape of his—"

"Four circuits, Lance Bombardier, till that grin has been removed. Utterly."

"He'll not make—"

"Four circuits. Full pack. At the double."

"He'll not manage it."

"You may stop the instant that grin is wiped from his spirit."

"Yes Bombardier. Okay, Smiley, Left, Right, Left!"

"Leave him! No hands. At the double!"

"Why did you permit him to take off his pack, Lance Bombardier?"

"He couldn't carry it any longer."

"My instruction was full pack and at the double."

"Yes Bombardier."

"At the double!"

"He can't, Bombardier."

"Can't?"

"Can't get up. He's passed out."

"Pick him up. Stand him on his feet. Head up. Show me his face. Quick. Ah, still grinning. Boy, do you hear me?"

"He's out, Bombardier."

"Hold him. Do you hear me, boy? I'm waiting. That's better, eyes open at last. Do you—hell, get back, get off me! Get him off me! Lance Bomb—"

"Smiley—Christ, you . . ."

"That's done for him, Lance Bombardier—assault! Assault on parade. Lance Bombardier, pick him up. Up! Full pack—full pack! Four circuits—"

"There's no way, Bombardier—"

"Four circuits!"

"He'll not make thirty yards!"

"Four circuits. That soldier assaulted a superior rank! Do you hear me, Lance Bombardier?"

"Yes Bombardier."

"Well?"

"He'll not go no further, Bombardier."

"Pick him up."

"He's dead, Bombardier."

"Dead?"

"Fetch a doctor if you want, but he's gone."

"Turn him over. Impossible."

"It's happened. He's dead."

"No way!"

"Dead, Bombardier."

"Fetch the camp doctor . . . Boy, you're faking. Get up. Get him up, you two!"

"Not faking, Bombardier."

"Faking I said, Lance Bombardier. Look. Look at him. Dead bodies don't grin like that."

Choices

"You want to take him now, Lieutenant?"

The Security car had been parked since midday opposite the apartment block beside the old Catholic church in Gorky Street.

"Let him have his walk. You never know, he may come back with the manuscript tucked underneath his arm."

"What about his daughter, Lieutenant?"

"She is his weak link."

The man at the wheel of the Security car looked at his superior. She scared him.

For weeks now Zelda had considered betraying her father. Today, she had made up her mind.

"Zelda, I'm going out for a walk. Will you do the usual for me—hide Boris Fourteen under the Three Wise Men?"

"What if I'm caught with it on the stairs?"

"They don't search juveniles."

There had only been the two of them, Boris and Zelda, since Karyn, Zelda's stepmother, had died eleven months ago. Her death had crippled them both, at first bringing father and daughter closer, but gradually the way each reacted to her death proved a barrier between them.

Boris had escaped more and more into his fictions: his writing had always been an obsession Karyn and Zelda had resented. It closed him off from them. Karyn had often said, "You care more for your fictional characters, Boris, than those you're supposed to love."

Boris always reacted heatedly. "That's nonsense."

"Then why do you spend more time with the people in your pages than you do with us?"

"I'll come for a walk with you, Dad," said Zelda. "It's so stuffy in here."

He had not expected Zelda to join him. "Better not. It isn't exactly a fresh-air walk."

It was one of *those* walks. Hush-hush, during which conspiracies took shape; for to be a writer in this country at this time was to invite danger.

Zelda resented Boris's obsession with his fictions less than Karyn had done; less, that is, than she resented the danger Boris's writings caused for everyone around him.

This was her case against him: "You put us all at risk."

"It's a risk worth taking," Boris argued. "To speak the truth."

"For you it might be worth it."

Boris had taken Boris Fourteen from the bottom shelf of the kitchen cupboard, its temporary hiding place between baking dishes. Naming his works in this way had become a family joke: Boris Ten had started the troubles. It was a story about a factory worker who wrote a letter to his superiors informing them of faulty machinery. When nothing was done to repair the machinery, the man had written to a member of the government who had spoken on television about efficiency being a priority of state.

The man had lost his job.

Not a very exciting story, but it was considered sufficiently controversial to be refused publication by the censor. After the script had been returned to Boris by the magazine, the phone-taps began.

At first Boris had been shocked that Security were listening in to his telephone conversations, then it pleased him: "It means that what I am writing is gathering in importance."

Boris Eleven and Twelve were playscripts. They were neither performed nor printed though they were widely circulated in samizdat—carbon copies to friends and friends of friends, one of whom was a friend of Security.

Boris lost his job in the high school. He was asked to look for new accommodation. From having a room with a view over the park, Zelda found herself in a bedroom above an ugly yard full of bins and broken-doored garages. There was no space to put up the poster Karyn had given her of New York's Empire State Building, taken from the air.

The morning Zelda had found a dead cockroach in her slipper Boris had announced, "I've acquired a tail. There are two of them, in plain clothes, following me wherever I go." He had been amused. "What a tribute to a poor scribbler!"

Boris Thirteen had been written as a comedy. It turned out to be a tragedy. It was a one-act play, a skit on the inefficiencies and dishonesties of bureaucracy: it seemed to imply that the more power an official is given, the more corrupt that person becomes.

First there had been a reading of the play in the home of an activist for civil rights. Security must have been sleeping on the job. Emboldened, Boris and his friends planned a production with professional actors.

Unlucky thirteen, for the performance was raided halfway through. The actors, the audience of thirty-five and the author were arrested and taken for questioning.

While Karyn and Zelda waited in the police station for news of what was to happen to Boris, Security had visited their flat and ransacked it.

They had stripped every room. Cupboard drawers had been upturned on the floor. Shelves were swept clean so that everything that was breakable broke; and the devastation had so upset Karyn that she lay in a darkened room for days with the worst migraine of her life. Even when the massive headache had passed, she had refused to touch anything in the apartment, refused even to dress herself in the clothes which Security had handled, cast in all directions, trodden on.

Zelda had had to go out and buy new clothes. She discovered, on her errands, that the raid had become common property. Everybody she knew signalled their knowledge of it, though rarely in so many words.

It was at that time that Zelda's boyfriend Jiri, a bright boy with a future in the local government office, stopped seeing her. He did not give any reason and she did not ask for one. She knew.

Boris's first words after the raid had been, "I've lost everything." He was referring to his precious manuscripts, especially his latest play, Boris Fourteen, for public consumption entitled *Open Prison*. He had been working on it for a year.

Karyn had said, "You've still got us, or do we not count?"

He had sat with his head in his hands and wept. Three weeks later Karyn took an overdose. She went to the park. She sat under the bridge where the swans pass; she left no note—something Boris had found impossible to understand:

"Why couldn't she just explain it, tell us why?"

Zelda had stared at her father compassionately, but amazed. I don't think you even begin to understand how real people tick. She did not put such thoughts into words. Instead, she asked, "Will you write about Karyn?"

Boris had not appeared to have considered Karyn as a character in one of his plays. He had stared out over the roofs of the town. There had been an early sprinkling of snow. "The French painter, Monet, did a portrait of his wife the moment she expired." He had sighed. "Artists are cold fish. I don't know. Karyn was too close."

"Too close?" It was not the way Zelda perceived things.

Boris' thoughts had slipped to his other loss: "I was a damnfool not to keep a copy of *Open Prison*. It was the best thing I'd ever done."

Zelda dared to say, "Perhaps it's time you tried something else. Paint pictures or something."

Boris had not been listening. "I must get down to it again. Clear my thoughts."

Zelda heard her own forlorn voice: "What's the point? You'll write it, the Security will come for it. We'll be moved on. There'll be no place at College for me. And no job."

For months there had been a truce between them; and beneath the daily exchanges of life on the surface, a deep silence.

Instead of bringing father and daughter into closer understanding and closer union, Karyn's death made Boris more the hermit than he had ever been. He worked day and night on his re-write of *Open Prison*.

Witnessing her father's obsession which commanded all his time and his thoughts, Zelda suffered loneliness. "I am less important," she thought, "than a load of marks on paper."

This morning he had been full of good cheer. His script was finished. He insisted on a toast to its completion. He poured Zelda a full glass of Scotch whisky. He raised his glass:

"I reckon this play will get me put inside once and for all. If I smuggle a copy abroad, there's a chance of publication and production."

"And that will be worth a year in prison?"

"No. But it's a risk I've got to take."

"Why?"

"You don't know?"

"Tell me."

"Zelda, my pet, one day the scales will fall from your eyes."

"I hope so." She insisted, "But in the meantime, tell me why it's worth it?"

For the first time in weeks, Boris paid his daughter full attention, though this did not reduce his defensiveness: "Tell me this, Zelda, will anything I say convince you?"

"It might."

"And I say it won't. Your heart's closed against it, be honest." He had triumphed. There would be no gain in lying.

She answered by holding out her hands for the manuscript in its buff folder. "If that's the case, are you being wise to trust me?"

"Lieutenant," said the driver of the Security car which had become powdered with fresh snow, "even with promises you can't keep, how are you going to make this girl believe you? It's her only parent she'll be shopping, remember."

"She'll believe me because I'm a woman, and—"

"And?"

"Because it makes sense."

The driver grinned. "Meaning—it's women who have their feet on the ground?"

"You could say that."

The driver tapped the steering wheel. "Whichever way you put it, it's betrayal."

"You men—you live on empty words."

No one owned a car to put in the garages behind the apartment block, except Vassezck in Flat One whom everyone suspected was the local eyes and ears of Security.

Zelda's route with her father's manuscript took her to the garage of Old Leila, the widow at number forty-five. This was crammed to the iron rafters with religious woodcarvings done by Leila's husband. Neighbours used to say the carver was buried among his statuettes to save on funeral costs.

Zelda feared the Room of the Statues. The faces of saints and martyrs, of angels and devils pierced the gloom, row upon row of them in flung confusion; many scarcely visible for the black veils of spiders' webs. Merely to open the garage door meant touching generations of dead flies and moths, snapping the matted cords to gain a space, brushing them off hand and arm, shoulder, cheek and hair.

Dad's mind made much of Leila's place. He had once spoken of the statuettes as a sleeping army, ready at a certain call to rise up and march through the streets.

As usual, Zelda's response had disappointed him:

"They're just ugly lumps of wood. They're rubbish and Leila ought to be made to burn them."

Boris had thrown a temper. "You astound me. Once, statues like those fetched high prices. They were treasured, worshipped. People lit candles before them, knelt and prayed in front of them—and you'd burn them?"

"Who wants to live in the past?"

"The past is what makes us, Zelda." He had paused, wondering whether the argument was worth pressing on with. "Tell me something—what icons will this generation leave behind it?"

"Icons?"

"Things people revere. That have a value beyond themselves. What will your generation leave behind?"

Zelda had scored a bull's-eye with her retort, "There won't be any room, Dad, because of all your manuscripts bunging up the place and gathering mouse droppings."

He had taken it well. "Of course. And all of them unread."

She had shown no mercy. "Does it matter?"

"To me it matters. I'm only sorry it doesn't seem to matter to you."

"*I* don't matter, do I?"

The snow was falling again. A wind carried it inwards past Zelda, freezing her legs. She was angry. She gazed around the statuettes, each imprisoned in a mesh of webs, some rotted into straggly black pigtails. There was St Peter with cracked halo and flaking forehead; a bored looking St Sebastian whose body seemed none the worse for being punctured with arrows. There was St Catherine sugar-smiling on the spikes of her wheel.

"You fools," said Zelda. It seemed an appropriate comment. "I've had enough of you lot and I've had enough of this." She held up Boris's manuscript. Written on it in bold black letters were the words:

DOMESTIC ACCOUNTS

That would make a better title to the play, Zelda thought. To call it *Open Prison* is to ask for trouble; call it *Domestic Accounts* and they'd probably let it be put on in the capital, with the politburo all lined up in the front row.

Complimentary tickets, of course.

Because of the snow outside, the Room of the Statues was almost cheerfully bright. Some snow had come in from a broken windowpane. It rested on the head of St Bernard, patron of the lost. A drop of water hung from his nose and made Zelda laugh.

"Well, Bernie," she said aloud—it was a habit she had

fallen into since Jiri had abandoned her as an undesirable acquaintance—"at least there's something about you that's real. Which is more than can be said for the characters in this." She wagged the manuscript. "I think he must come down here for his inspiration."

An inner voice hinted that she might be being unfair. "Of course I'm being unfair. That's what I want to be. It's my right!"

She turned, tripped on the plump calf of a kneeling angel and fell straight into the assembled host. Spiders' webs disintegrated. Statues clattered into one another and Boris's manuscript slipped from its buff protector and scattered over the dark floor.

Zelda rubbed the arm she had fallen on. She sat up. "I just hope he's numbered the pages." She gathered the typewritten sheets and discovered that there were two scripts—one, the play, neatly stapled at the corner; the other, something Boris had never mentioned. It was a sheaf of handwritten pages.

Zelda was curious. Boris's play did not interest her, he had talked about it so much; but her sudden eagerness to check the contents of this mystery script indicated that Zelda was less indifferent to her father's works than she professed to be.

The first page bore no title, only a question-mark inside a circle. She was astonished at what she read:

For weeks now, Catriona had considered betraying her father. Today, she had made up her mind.

"Catriona?" her father had said, "I am going out for a walk. Will you do the usual for me, hide Deposit Account Item Fourteen under the Three Wise Men?"

"What if I'm caught with it on the stairs?"

"They don't search juveniles."

There had only been the two of them since Tanya, Catriona's mother, had died eleven months before . . .

Zelda reacted as though she had jammed her fingers in a live electric socket. It was uncanny, not only to be written about, but her thoughts and her feelings predicted.

In Dad's mind I'm already a traitor.

She read on, exactly what she knew, exactly what had happened: this Catriona had been sent to hide a precious manuscript in a storeroom belonging to an old widow. The storeroom contained—well, there was no need to describe what it contained.

"Plainly he expected me to find this, and read it. How could he be so certain?"

"Writers," Boris had once said, "are beachcombers, hoarding everything that's curious till one day they find a perfect place for it."

So Dad had hoarded up this damp room crammed with images of the past, of a dead age; he had taken Zelda/Catriona to it; he had provided the place with sufficient illumination to stir enough seedlings of magic to make the messenger pause amid the dumb statues.

He had also caused Catriona, as well as Zelda, to tumble over among the saints and discover the secret manuscript.

"But for my name, I am one of my father's characters." This was not in the script.

She touched her eyes. They were open.

Catriona touched her eyes. They were open. "I could be dreaming," she said.

Zelda lay aside the manuscript. If I'm dreaming, it's not my dream. It's Boris's dream, his wish. She smiled, troubled but intrigued. Perhaps to him I only exist as Catriona. If I can become one of his fictions, I might become real to him.

Then he might love me.

Zelda returned to the tale of her other self:

Catriona wondered if she was somehow being tested out. Was her father prompting her to make a move by giving her the one copy of the play which meant so much to him; was he challenging her to decide whose side she was on?

Zelda addressed her absent father: "It's nothing to do with taking sides."

"It's nothing to do with taking sides," protested Catriona. Oh. Point made.

Catriona's father had said to his friend Stefan, "She'll betray me. That is what the world has come to, at least in this country."

Thanks, Boris, for your trust.

Was this really a test, wondered Zelda, an experiment in which a trap was baited? At this moment, Security could be waiting outside his door: what then?

It suddenly occurred to her how little she had read of her father's work. For Zelda, what he wrote was as private as the priest's confessional. He disappeared into his room for hours on end, days on end, then he would go for a walk or a drink or to meet his literary friends.

He might as well have been doing jigsaw puzzles. Zelda did not care for jigsaw puzzles; they seemed as pointless as writing stories that would never be published, plays that would never be performed.

She read on:

Of her father, she knew only one side. She knew of his temper, his bouts of frustrated shouting, his sore-headedness; his petty complaints. She knew nothing—and cared nothing —of the Other Self that laboured with profound love to capture the essence of things and to share with others . . .

Zelda stopped reading.

Catriona stopped reading.

"Any more of this and I'll be shedding crocodile tears."

Zelda thought, Why didn't Dad just sit me down at the table and have a chat? Instead, he writes me into a story; he sends me down among the statues so if I get angry at what he says he won't be around while I poke him in the eye with "the essence of things".

The next paragraph Zelda agreed with:

Having a father who sat at a desk chewing a pen or rattling the keys of an old typewriter was a bore in comparison with seeing him conduct an orchestra, point to a building he had designed, play Hamlet or King Lear on stage or, best of all, chat to celebrities on television.

It was nothing. A real state of the null and void.
Yet had Catriona been unfair?

Here we go, thought Zelda, Dad's feeling sorry for himself. He is going to write about how he is neglected and misunderstood; how nobody seems to care whether he writes or dies. The old old song.

No, Catriona had not been unfair.

Zelda laughed; he's getting generous in his old age. What had Catriona been, then? She turned the page.

Catriona sat among the statues. She shivered with the late afternoon cold. She gathered up the pages of the play, neatly stapled in one corner. She got thoughtfully to her feet.

Yet, if not unfair, what had Catriona been? It was perhaps time for some home-truths . . .

The script abruptly ended. Zelda got thoughtfully to her feet. She shivered, yes, with the late afternoon cold. Had Dad left off the manuscript deliberately at this point? Did he want Zelda/Catriona to go on from here and decide what home-truths had to be faced?

Zelda hid the manuscript of the play, and the unfinished

Confessional of Catriona, in the usual place—beneath a triple statuette of the Wise Men from the East; an addition to their precious gifts of gold, frankincense and myrrh.

A gift of hope to the hopeful. Where did she recall that phrase? Ah, two birthdays ago, when Boris had written her a poem in a birthday greetings card. In the move from the old place, Zelda had lost the card, but that one line she had not forgotten:

A gift of hope to the hopeful.

She had liked it, though it did not seem to mean much. Boris had asked about the poem. "Did you keep it?"

"I kept it."

He had waited; wanted her to speak of it as a treasure, like Mother's lock of hair which she had encapsulated as a child in a mould of clear plastic.

"Because I didn't keep a copy."

She had been silent for a moment, then asked, "Do you remember, Dad, that English poet who put his verses in the grave with his dead lover, and then had second thoughts and had the grave dug up again so he could get his poems back?"

"I remember."

Father and daughter had interpreted the story in different ways. He had sympathised with the poet; Zelda had looked upon the poet's action as a doublecross: those poems meant more to him than his dead lover had done. "You'd not sacrifice your plays for me, would you, Dad?"

"Sacrifice them? What do you mean?"

"Burn them, say—if I asked you."

"What would be the point?"

"Would you do it—to save my life, for example?"

"Well of course." He had added briskly, "How could such a situation arise?"

"To save me from arrest, would you?"

"Would I what?"

"Destroy all your manuscripts?"

He replied that her mother had asked him the same thing;

so had Karyn. "Why are you women so competitive?" he asked.

"Women aren't—"

"They want to come first in everything. Don't violinists hear the old cry, 'I'm always second fiddle?' And why only blame artists? What about bankers or sportsmen or mountain climbers?"

Zelda remembered Karyn's response in an identical argument:

"That, Boris, makes my point!"

The afternoon had darkened with a flurry of snow, some of it blown by a sharp wind from off the roof and guttering above.

Zelda thought, how would Catriona's story continue? Those remarks about sacrificing precious manuscripts for human life ought to go in. Yes. And, how about:

She was thinking of how one of her father's painter friends had posed a similar problem, and stirred a nightful of talk among the clan who gathered in the flat every other Friday night.

"If your house was burning down, and you could rescue a Rembrandt masterpiece or a cat—but not both—what would you decide?"

Such evenings Zelda recollected with pleasure. When artists put aside their lonely pursuits and came together, there was fun. On this occasion there was much debate about the value of the life of a cat; about the pleasure a hundred generations would derive from gazing at the rescued Rembrandt.

Now how did it go?

Finally the artist who had raised the question about the fire, the Rembrandt and the cat, said, "Giacometti the sculptor posed the question. He decided he would rescue life rather than art."

Shall I write in Dad's reply? Here's how it was:

Catriona's father had been cynical. "That," he had said, "is because Giacometti was talking in principle, all things weighed and considered. In the panic of the moment when the fire was raging, he might have chosen otherwise. After all, one Rembrandt could rescue a million other unfortunate cats."

Catriona had leapt up in protest. She was livid. She had stormed into the kitchen, shouting, "No Rembrandt is worth a cat's tail!"

Well that's what I thought of doing, confessed Zelda. She admired Catriona her guts. In reality Zelda had sat dumbly hugging her knees; but:

From that moment Catriona decided she was the cat in a story where the fire had not yet started.

"I like that," Zelda said aloud. "Perhaps Dad's test is for me to complete the story."

The concrete stairs to the apartment were covered in snow brought in by many feet; it had not been there when Zelda had left the building.

Four storeys. There were heads peering out of doors at the commotion above. Boris had refused entry to Security and they had battered the door in.

"It's that clerk on the fourth," said one curious woman to a query from her husband. She had just washed her hair and wore a yellow plastic bag over it. "I said he was trouble."

Not wearing a coat, with no friends to go to for refuge in this part of the city and with no money in her pocket, Zelda saw no alternative but to continue up the stairs. I guess Boris would have written me as turning back and hiding in the Room of the Statues.

As a result, Catriona was shielded from the brutality of the raid . . . Thus the manuscript was saved.

"And my only meal ticket in this whole world snatched off to gaol. Not likely."

She hesitated on the angle of the stairs to the third floor. I have to be certain I know what I am doing. I will tell them, if they lay off my father they can have his script.

They could also have, as a bonus for going away and not returning, a truckful of ideologically unsound religious statuettes.

Boris had been momentarily silenced by a blow across the face; a sleeved blow which drew no blood. "Sit!" The blow had come from a short, plump Security man with black hair on the back of his hands, but the command came from a woman, tallish even on flat heels, hair cut short but stylishly enough to make it attractive.

Other Security men were dismembering the flat with a thoroughness which would render it uninhabitable in future.

"Tell me where the manuscript is, Boris," said the Lieutenant, "and we can stop the damage immediately."

Zelda turned on the stairs. It had been a horrible mistake to come up so far. She gasped, for a Security man was right behind her. She stumbled. He checked her with one arm and thrust her on up the stairs.

"Our little messenger, I think, Lieutenant."

Boris threw up his hands in dismay at the sight of Zelda. "Why didn't you make yourself scarce?"

"Hands on the table," ordered the chubby Security man. He had a pistol. It threw a shadow over the table. "Hands!" Still with his eyes firing questions at Zelda, Boris did as he was told, placing his white, gentle hands flat on the dining room table.

The Lieutenant waved Zelda into a seat opposite her father. She addressed Zelda. "Hands tell you so much, don't you think, Zelda?"

Zelda stared down at her own hands. They had good shape but they were spoilt by ugly warts which had sprouted between her fingers in recent months. She remained silent.

"Will you please order your men to observe the laws of the land?" appealed Boris.

"We have a search warrant. Do you wish to see it?"

"You know what I mean. I've told you, there's no manuscript."

"*Open Prison*, that is what we are after and what we intend to find."

"You already have it."

"You did not learn your lesson. You wrote it again. It has been circulated in samizdat. We want it."

"That is quite untrue. It has never been circulated."

"Then you admit there is a second version?"

Zelda stared at her father. He was digging his own grave.

"No," he asserted, "there is no second version. And no copy. That's the end for *Open Prison* for the present."

Zelda asked herself, If you were the Lieutenant, would you believe that?

The Lieutenant waited, letting the sounds of the search in Boris's bedroom-study do her answering for her. There was a crash of metal. "Your typewriter, I think. Do you possess a licence for that machine?"

Boris replied, "It is ludicrous that you have to have permission to own a typewriter."

"It is the law of the land."

"It's a stupid law."

"Every time you open your mouth, Boris, you condemn the State."

There was another crash. The bookshelves were down, being wrenched away from the wall. Another searcher was in the kitchen, stripping the cupboards, prising off doors. Zelda could see him through the open door. He was going through the contents of the small fridge which broke down a few days ago. It would never work again for the Security man was taking the mechanism apart.

Zelda had been impressed by the way Boris had so far kept his temper. Now he acted more the way she saw him, choosing the wrong company and the wrong time to blurt out his thoughts:

"Why do you hound us? I love this country, I love its people. Yet you treat me as a traitor."

"If you are not a traitor, if you are an honest writer—"

"Yes, that's exactly what I am—an honest writer!"

"If you are what you say you are, why do you have to pass your manuscripts round in secret?"

Zelda perceived the trap, but Boris did not. He exploded with anger: "Secret? You think we really want to do everything in secret? You understand nothing. Nothing!"

"Hands!" commanded the chubby Security man, striking a match on his pistol-grip, then feeding a cigarette into his mouth with his left hand.

"That's rich," went on Boris. "You refuse us the freedom to publish and then you accuse us of treason—"

"Dad!" Zelda could take no more of this. "You are making things worse for us."

The Lieutenant turned her severe blue eyes on Zelda; but it was an agreeable look she gave her. "Your father does seem in need of good advice, Zelda. Who is Catriona, by the way?"

Zelda felt a chill pass through her body. She stared at her father as the Lieutenant continued, "You are writing a diary to Catriona, Boris?"

"Why ask questions?" replied Boris calmly. "You seem to know all the answers already." He smiled. He was misbehaving again. "Except where exactly these manuscripts are to be found."

The Lieutenant stared not into Boris's eyes but above them, where the hair receded from his forehead. "We have all day and all night," she said, her voice cold, dry, meticulous. "And in prison we have for ever."

Zelda was no stranger to fear, yet now she felt it so acutely the blood in her veins seemed to become solid. All activity seemed to concentrate on the pulse in her throat. The Lieutenant had turned to her.

"Look at me, Zelda. Not at your hands. That's better. Your warts are possibly due to anxiety. For it is an anxious life, isn't it, being the daughter of a wanted man?"

"Say nothing, Zelda," Boris instructed her. "You are under no obligation. This matter is nothing to do with you."

"Nothing?" interrupted the Lieutenant. Once more she paused to let the sounds of the Security search express themselves. "This is Zelda's home as well as yours, is it not? I am afraid her own room will not be spared."

It was a shock when the Lieutenant shouted, "Is there anything yet?"

The searchers paused in their work: "Nothing, Lieutenant."

Zelda, disobeying orders and staring tenaciously at her hands, heard:

"But there is a choice. You both have a choice."

A choice: where had she heard that before?

"Is human life, a livelihood, worth less," asked the Lieutenant, directly of Zelda, "than a work of fiction?"

A Rembrandt, should it be rescued from the burning house before a cat?

It had been a day of uncanny overlaps and strange resonances, so it was only with mild surprise that Zelda heard the Lieutenant ask, "Did you ever hear about the problem posed by the sculptor Giacometti? In a burning house, which would you choose to rescue first—a priceless Rembrandt or a mangy cat?"

Zelda decided, One of Boris's so-called friends has told the Security everything. They'll even know we serve coffee from Nicaragua; they will know about the secret codes of Boris and his friends—three rings of the phone for safety, four for danger; of how a note on white paper signifies the opposite, one on green means what it says. They will know addresses and phone numbers; meeting places when circumstances were not threatening; rendezvous points when the pressure was on from Security. They would know the secret 'postboxes' for messages, and they would know the messenger.

Zelda was a party to all this. Her complicity was known. "Do not look away, young lady," warned the Lieutenant with misleading gentleness. "Of course you realise all this involves you."

Boris began to protest. "Hands!" bellowed the chubby Security man as Boris attempted to gesticulate.

"Your daughter is involved, and liable."

Liable?

Boris was distant, fighting for inner control, listening to warning voices, thus the Lieutenant's next question took him off guard. "As a writer, you would wish for the freedoms of the West, am I right?"

Boris nodded, uncertain. "Freedom to speak out, yes."

"Freedom to corrupt people's minds in pursuit of wealth?"

Zelda sensed she would have no control over the fear that was engulfing her. She was involved, yes—but liable? Could they arrest her? The thought of being locked away, of being interrogated, beaten perhaps; of her hair being shorn, of being made to dress in criminals' clothes, of being fed meat and potato scraps swimming in cold gravy—yes, she had read all about it from Dad's books, heard all about it from his friends who had been released from prison; the thought made her shake so visibly that the chubby Security man laughed silently.

An expert in hands, he watched Zelda's with special interest.

The Lieutenant was saying, "We should give you the liberty to join your friends in the West. Then you will discover what real freedom there is." She came behind Zelda. She placed her hands on her shoulders as though presenting daughter to father. "Should we offer him that freedom, Zelda?"

Zelda shook, but did not speak.

"You plainly share my doubts, for your father is a very serious writer. There is substance in his work. It is not easy. In fact it requires a considerable effort of concentration to appreciate."

Boris was rather flattered.

"It is why *we* take him seriously."

Once more he rose to the bait: "You mean in the West they wouldn't take me seriously, is that it?"

"They would toast you for a while as they do all exiles from our country. They will interview you on radio or even television. There will be one or two learned articles about you—and then they will abandon you." She smiled. "While here, we are always interested in you, Boris."

She did not let him reply. "The liberty the West would offer you, Boris, is the liberty to be ignored."

"That'd be something."

"Would it? Surely you crave for attention?"

"Only for my work."

"Don't split hairs, Boris. Your work is you. For that you will risk everything—even your own daughter's safety and well-being."

"No!"

The Lieutenant took her time in replying. "Whose hands are on the table? Yours alone?"

Boris retreated far into himself. He spoke mechanically in a voice that almost died away. "There is no manuscript. You are wasting my time. My daughter is not involved. There's no liability . . ."

Zelda's own hands had stopped shaking. She saw that Dad would not rescue her; not merely because it was probably beyond his power to do so, but because it was beyond his will.

At this instant, Zelda read the circumstances entirely from the point of view of her own survival. She was aware of this. For Boris, arrest and imprisonment were an affirmation of his existence—his existence as a writer. The fact that he was behind bars for a cause he deemed noble, as a sign of courage, would buoy him up in the bleak days of his future.

The Lieutenant also read the circumstances of this instant. With timing that seemed to indicate that she had written this scene in her head before enacting it, the Lieutenant came round to the front of Zelda. She placed her own hands in front of Zelda's, almost fingertip to fingertip:

"Tell me where the manuscript is, Zelda, and you will go free."

The words brought Boris out of his place of retreat. "Say nothing, Zelda! You are not involved, you are not liable—they are just kidding you on."

Again the Lieutenant chose the right words and the right time. "Rembrandt and the cat, Zelda. You know how your father will choose. Now you must choose."

As from another person's lips, Zelda asked, "What will happen?"

"To you, nothing."

Boris fought. "No, Zelda! If you give them what they want, they'll demand more and more. It will never be enough. They will harry you for ever and ever."

The Lieutenant's voice was utterly calm. The sounds of searching for the hidden manuscript had stopped as if the Security men realised that it had already been found. "Zelda, or should I say Catriona? Your father will always be in our sights. He knows that. In fact he wants it. But you deserve to be free of us." She turned her head slowly. "And perhaps free of him."

Zelda eased back her chair. She stood up.

"No, Zelda," implored Boris; strangely, though, with less passion than she would have expected. She walked away from her father, towards the door.

"I just want to be free of it," she said. The guard at the apartment entrance stood aside for her.

Catriona felt only darkness, yet her fear had subsided. She would betray her father not because it was for his good or for hers, but because until she had done so, nothing would ever be clear between them.

"This way," she said.

Sir Les Of The Windmills

"Offside!"

"Penalty!"

"Send her off, Ref!"

Jan Rickards had hit a two past square-leg. As she and Ali McGuire, team captain, had crossed each other leisurely for the second time, the barracking from the boundary rail turned to ironic cheers.

"Give her a medal!"

"Wi'legs like hers she's gotta be a stripper!"

"She's blushing!"

"Blacks don't blush."

The Hartleywood Women's XI did not usually draw more than a pocketful of spectators. Now there were sixteen of them—ten supporters, a mix of relatives and friends, plus team coach George Sowerby, once a minor counties player.

The barrackers were five teenage motor cyclists who had marked their entry to the cricket field with a triple circuit before coming to a noisy halt beside the pavilion.

This was Hartleywood's last match before their week's tour, an annual event organised by Ali, a former England player.

Jan had only been playing cricket for a season, though at school she had always wanted to have a go; watching Test Matches on TV, especially coverage of the winter tour, had cast a spell on a lonely but fiercely independent girl. Out of sorts with her job, her family and often herself, Jan saw cricket as a sort of magic carpet unrolled once a week for her to escape the oppressive routine of six o'clock in the morning starts at the bakery, bitter rows with Desmond her married brother and the imprisoning streets of the city. These Jan exchanged for quiet meadows, the comradeship of her teammates and the fascination of a game of many skills.

Today she had reached her highest score—twenty-seven, and the cries of the motor cyclists were a sudden upset to her concentration. She played forward to the next ball and missed it by a bat's width. The one that followed struck her on the front pad. There was a loud appeal for leg before wicket from the fielders, and a double chorus from the bike boys:

"Give her a tennis racket!"

"She's no backlift!"

"Wag it about a bit, Pigtails!"

Laughter.

Jan was given Not Out by the umpire, and the over was complete before she could make any more errors. Pigtails! She took the opportunity as the bowling changed ends to stare at the pavilion, trying at the same time to take Ali's advice, "Ignore the Rent-a-Mob, and maybe they'll drift off to the paddling pool."

Pigtails—that really got her; and their cockiness. She felt like shouting, "Come and do better!" but she wasn't sure they would refuse the offer.

Ali scored a single off the first ball of the next over. She did not seem to interest the bikers.

"Keep a straight bat, Pigtails!"

"Play down the line of the ball!"

It was actually good advice. She patted her crease, "Show them," a voice urged her. The ball passed on her leg-side, harmlessly and beyond reach. Her best shots were on the offside, in particular her square-cut and cover-drive. She waited two more balls, dead-batting each into the pitch and with so little force that she fielded the ball herself.

"She needs harmone treatment!" The voice appeared to emanate from the youth on the red bike, with a red helmet dangling from the handlebars. He was the worst, she decided; she named him The Lip. She could sense him grinning, arms folded, just waiting for her to do something wrong.

Her image of him was taking swift shape: good looking, a swaggerer; he pulled all the birds, or boasted that he did.

And he's probably as thick as this bat.

The captain of the opposing team had rearranged the field slightly, moving square-leg further over towards cover and beckoning cover to take the extra-cover position. The delivery was short, quicker than the others in the over, and about a foot outside the off stump.

Jan had remembered—thanks, lads—to give herself time for a generous backlift. She angled the bat across the line of the ball, her left leg anchored centre crease, her right moving outwards and backwards. She felt the crack of willow against leather, that unique and joyful sound which denotes a perfectly timed shot.

The ball travelled sizzlingly through the air at waist height for ten yards, then dipped to ground. The outfield was dry, bouncy as cork, and the ball seemed to gather pace as it hurtled to the boundary and the pavilion.

"Best shot of my life," Jan thought, watching backward-point give half-hearted chase. The ball struck the white boundary board directly in front of the five hecklers. It bounced viciously and evidently with relish.

Yes, the first masterpiece in Janine Rickards' short career as an artist of the willow (to borrow George Sowerby's proud words above the home team applause). The ball could not have done sweeter service: it went for the Red Bike and Red Bike was too slow to dodge.

Result, a shattered front light.

This made four friends for Jan out of the five bikers. They whooped, clapped and cheered. Yet what amused them most—a fact unknown to Jan—was that the unhappy victim had been the only one not to have taken part in the heckling.

All the while he had remained silent. Perhaps it was

this which annoyed his friends. The broken lamp proved something—that life's not fair. It was a liberating discovery.

Now the offended youth did speak out: "Hey! You'll have to pay for this." His words were met with laughter; in any case Jan was too far away to hear. She acknowledged the response to her square-cut with a modest wave of the bat.

And was clean bowled by the last delivery of the over.

This was Jan's first real applause as she returned to the pavilion. "Great stuff!" "Great bit of stuff!" The bikers—bar one—were overdoing things as might be expected. "Stick her up the order!" "Pick her for the West Indies!" "How about a bit of leg before wicket, Honey!" Only The Lip remained silent.

Jan took off her pads; a great feeling, this. "Off my own bat"—she liked that phrase. Now it meant something to her. She was back with the ball rising; she relived the moment—a swift backlift, feet angled (the world at your feet, absolutely) and then crack; there was no describing the pleasure as eye and arm and body selected the choicest moment.

"She's coming over, Les."

"She gonna wop you."

"Or coach him in strokeplay."

"Love them short skirts. What you think, Les?"

Jan kept a civil distance. "I'm sorry about the lamp." He was silent, gone as red as his helmet. "It wasn't intentional. Fact is," she smiled, "I'd no idea I could hit the ball that hard."

"My friend thinks you're a bloke in disguise," said the true lip, who introduced himself as Neil.

A close-up view of Jan killed the joke. Neil was almost apologetic. "Course, that's because Les is scared of girls."

"I'm not."

"You're a kid!"

"Anyway," said Jan, "I'm sorry."

"Nothing," stammered Les.

"Sorry?"

"He's dumb."

"I'm not dumb."

"Prove you're not." Neil turned back to Jan, asked her her name. "You're not from these parts."

When he was told, Neil responded, "That's where your racials riot, isn't it? You're not a racial rioter, are you, Doll? Here, hang about, don't walk away when you're being talked to."

Les spoke up: "Leave off, Neil."

"You what?"

"Leave off."

Jan had checked her stride, then turned again towards the pavilion. Neil tried harder: "Dummy here wants to know why there's no cricket teams specially for birds down Brixton way."

Les said he didn't want to know.

"Course you do!"

Jan advanced a step. She had thought badly of Les, and unfairly. Now she liked him. "If you lived in the Smoke all week, you'd appreciate a trip out to all this." A slow and elegant movement of her outstretched arm invited the bikers to admire their own landscape—the deep green cricket meadow bordered with trees, and the gently rising, blue-shaded hills to west and north.

"I'd have thought you'd have preferred something hotter," replied Neil. "Wi' palm trees and that."

"I'm English. Born and bred." There was a challenge in Jan's voice. "Am I not supposed to enjoy my own countryside?"

"Oh yes!" The eagerness with which Les supported Jan's challenge made the others laugh. With his next move, he had them doubled up. He fished a scrap of paper from the pocket of his leather jacket. "Can I have your autograph, please?"

The match had lumbered on into the dusk, ending in a draw just before it became impossible to see the ball against the shadowy haycocks in adjoining fields. Drinks had been served on the pavilion verandah and no one seemed in a hurry to head home from what had been an idyllic day.

With a bus, train and tube journey ahead of her, Jan always left first. She came round the pavilion corner to find Les waiting for her. Alone, upright, he seemed not to have moved a muscle since she had left him. It plainly caused him a considerable effort to force out the words, "You want a lift?" And they emerged as a croak, registering as "Yant a tift?"

She understood. She would not be like his friend Neil ("A tift, what's a tift when it's at home? Ha! Ha!"):

"Without a front light?"

"No, the light's still working. You just broke the glass."

"Why did you wait?"

"I just wanted to."

She was in two minds. The bus was often late; sometimes it did not arrive at all, and it was a twenty-minute walk to the station.

"You're not hiding your L-plates, are you?"

"I'm fully qualified. Honest." He grinned. "And if you want to see my birth certificate, my Health Card, my cub badges . . ." He broke off. He raised his arm. "I'm a bit diabetic so I've my instructions on this name tab."

"I don't know."

"Please."

"Okay, then. The station."

He took her cricket bag. He strapped it over the pannier of the bike. "No bat?"

"No bat."

"You ought to have your own bat."

"Do you know much about the game?"

"I'm no use at it. No use at anything, really. But I love watching. You were great."

At the station he took her bag on to the platform for her, and showed no inclination to leave before the train arrived. Jan appreciated this: on Saturday nights, being on her own, she was often harassed by jokers who felt it okay to vent their wit on a Black girl. Sometimes she was treated to what her old General Studies teacher at the Tech had called Dimwit; sometimes it was Harshwit; occasionally, Bestialwit.

"This place is a menace," said Les, catching her thoughts and justifying his presence. "Full of yobbos like Neil."

"Not your friend, then?"

"Neil thinks I'm a loony."

"Why?"

"Because I'm not as bright as he is. He hates me because I got the bike."

A northbound train arrived on the opposite platform. Les was recognised. Three heads jammed out of an open window. "Christ, Les Bums has got himself a Black bird!"

"How's she rattle, Les?"

"Steady with them lighted matches, Les!"

The new hecklers were ignored. The train pulled out. "Sorry," he said. "They were in my class last year."

She was tempted to ask about "them lighted matches", yet it was none of her business. Instead, she asked him if he had a job.

"Sort of. I work in my father's garage. He's training me."

"You like it?"

"I hate it."

"What do you want to do?"

The train swept away their conversation. She said, "Sorry again about the lamp."

He opened the train door for her. His face spread with a childlike happiness. "It was worth it." He put her bag on the rack. "But you've got to have your own bat." The train was moving. "I'll try and get you one."

Jan often thought of Les during the week—the image of him silent among the laughter of his not-so-close friends as her square-cut shattered his proud lamp; his waiting like a sad puppy for its absent master beside the twilit pavilion;

his puzzlement at the way, because of her colour and because she was practising a 'man's game', she attracted the disfavour of strangers.

I think he was beginning to feel what it's like to be me. She had never met a boy her own age who had made that discovery.

When the hired coach picked up the Hartleywood Women's XI outside the village hall at ten on the Saturday morning, Les Bottomley, alias Les Bums—poor soul— had been waiting on his bike. He didn't wave, merely stared at Jan as she arrived from the station in Alison McGuire's car. She smiled and, at this sign of recognition, he came to life. "Hello."

"Another reception committee?" She was flattered then surprised, for Les was holding out a cricket bat to her.

"It's not new. But Stuart Surridge bats are good."

"For me? But where—"

"It's mine."

"I can't."

"I'll never use it. And that's a waste. You know what it's called?—Excalibur." He waited. "King Arthur's sword. It smites the enemy." Here once more was the childlike smile, causing Jan to think, he's a dreamer.

Les proffered the handle of Excalibur, holding on to the blade. "But only one person in the whole world can draw the sword. Have a go."

The rest of the team had gathered round amiably to watch this performance. Jan gripped the handle of the bat. She tugged. It was an effort. At first the rock holding Excalibur would not give up its prize.

"Again."

The others joined in, "Again!"

There was a cheer as the rock surrendered to Jan's touch. She gripped the bat. It had a good weight, and balance; and a short handle, which she preferred. She lifted up the blade, turned it in the sun.

"Excalibur!"

"To smite your enemies. I've had a new grip put on."

Ten o'clock and the bus was ready to leave on its cross-stitching tour of the Marches—Gloucestershire, Herefordshire and Shropshire, with a match every day on what George Sowerby said were some of the loveliest village grounds in the country.

Once on board, and sitting with her room-mate Elaine, Jan noticed that Les's bike was loaded up with a canvas bag attached to the pillion with elastics, and tied on top of that was a camping stove. He also carried a bulging rucksack.

Elaine was intrigued. "Who's betting Jan's new fan club will be waiting for us when we arrive?"

Three hours later, and a hundred and twenty miles west, Les Bottomley was parked beside the pavilion of a picturesque ground surrounded on three sides with rhododendrons. A river marked the boundary on the fourth side which opened on to the town.

"If he gives you any aggro, Jan," said Alison protectively, "let me know right away. We can do without yobbos in tow."

Jan defended her fan club. "He's nice. Just at a loose end, I think."

George Sowerby knew the Bottomley family. He was troubled and cautious. "Go easy on the lad—his mother died in the winter. His Dad's rough on him, and young Les has done one or two silly things in the village since then. Getting him that bike seems to have calmed him down a bit."

"What I'd like to know," said Renée, the team wicket-keeper, "is whether it's Jan's legs he fancies or her leg-glance!"

Jan clarified: "My square-cut, actually." She was thinking, Les never mentioned his family; but losing his mum does explain, maybe, how bewildered he seems; kind of drifting and distant. It's so difficult to connect with him, like knowing what stroke you want to play but just not being able to time things properly.

Such thoughts preoccupied Jan at the crease, for her good

performance last Saturday had prompted Alison to try her as opening bat.

Les had leant his bike against an empty bench and now stood beside the sightscreen. "Do you want him moved?" called the umpire to Jan.

"Moved?"

"Away from the sightscreen?"

"Oh no," she smiled. The words darted out, unplanned: "He's my lucky mascot."

"Guard?"

"One leg, please."

"Right, batsman?"

Batsman? Bats*woman* if you please. "Right." Jan was musing, as the bowler approached the wicket with a rather clumsy, loping stride, what would her brother Desmond think of her new friend? Eat him for breakfast, probably.

"No whites," Desmond told his kids, and never without a hint of reproach at Jan, "no whites over that front doorstep."

"Bullshit," Des's wife Marilyn would say, "it's all bullshit you're big-talking, and you know it." Marilyn stood no nonsense from her London bus driver husband.

"Last bus home, last bus home, woman!" Des always incanted that message when the matter of Them and Us cropped up. "Last bus home, remember!" He was referring to his three days in hospital and four weeks off work as a result of an attack—on the last bus—by a gang of white youths.

"You're as bad as them for calling names. Didn't your white pals stop the buses for half a day in protest?"

"Sympathy don't remove these scars, woman."

"You don't 'woman' me."

Jan shuddered at the recollection of Des's scars. She remembered them exactly as they had looked once the stitches had been removed. She was not hostile like Des, unforgiving. But she was, from the core of her being, suspicious; eternally on guard.

I'll be like that all my life.

"If whites are nice to you," Des had claimed, "it's only because they want something you've got."

"Whites get pushed around the same as us."

"It's different. A whole lot different."

"Where's the difference?"

"Shut up, you stupid woman."

Marilyn on these occasions would laugh. "Go drive your bus." In four words so much seemed to be summed up: Go drive your bus. And with Des, it usually worked. He had nothing against buses; buses, he said, were Red. That absolved them from racial intolerance.

"Oh?" Marilyn would respond, determined as ever to have the last word, "and when your mean machine don't start, what do you call him?"

There was no need for Des to reply.

"White scum, eh?"

Jan had shaped up defensively but confidently to the first four balls of the over. The next one was way outside the leg stump and she went for it with a controlled swing, wrists turning as the bat aligned with the ball—just as George had coached her to do. The contact was firm, the timing almost perfect, and she heard the applause as the shining new ball bisected square-leg and mid-wicket and shot for the boundary.

She acknowledged the special applause from beside the sightscreen: feverish, overdone—naturally—as if she'd struck the winning runs in a test match. Yet it pleased her.

For Les, I'm becoming Champion the Wonder Horse.

She pushed the next ball for a single and then proceeded to take eight runs off the next over. What a feeling, I'm on song: this is what I'm good at. Me and Excalibur, we can conquer the world.

The next moment, pride got its comeuppance. She played late at a rising ball and nudged an easy catch to first-slip: a horrible groan emanated from beside the sightscreen, then a cheer, for first-slip fumbled the catch. The ball fell safely to earth.

"Head over the ball!" roared Les. "Move your legs!"

She steadied herself and the runs flowed—two to cover, a boundary down fine-leg, a three that sent mid-on racing desperately up the slope; and all the while Les Bottomley cheered and clapped.

As Jan's score mounted, Les moved round to the scoreboard. He had picked up an armful of numbers and broke the local custom—which was only to register the run total, the number of wickets that had fallen, and the score of the last man, woman or person. Les was hanging up Jan's personal tally. What's more, he was behaving like a tic-tac man at the races, holding Jan's score above his head and displaying it to all points of the ground: 25; 29; 31 . . .

Les's delight at Jan's run-getting began to influence both match and spectators; the players tried harder, the spectators clapped louder. The excitement spread across the river and drew the attention of people at a small open-air market. Particularly attracted was a group of men who'd been drinking in the garden of a riverside pub until closing time. Loaded with beer cans, the men crossed the bridge on to the cricket ground and saw Jan hook a full toss for four to complete her first-ever fifty.

They witnessed a youth next to the scoreboard leaping in the air, shouting himself hoarse. They saw him sprint on to the field, dodge the square-leg umpire and hold up the Black woman's bat and arm.

"Effing prat!"

The four men were in their twenties, possibly older; they seemed to have been to the same barber, who had back-and-sided them with blunt shears. They each wore jeans and sleeveless shirts, one emblazoned with a death's head, two with the union jack and the fourth sporting the words ENGLISH SPOKEN.

Immediately they set up a rival vocal faction to Les Bottomley's one-man band of support. They assessed the bowling as being soft as ice cream: "Pitch it up, darlin', or it won't reach the wicket!" They derided every error in the fielding: "Ged off your knees, Short Arse!" They yelled fat jokes at Renée who admitted she was overweight, but not quite the Two Ton Tessie she was soon being called.

Most of the flak concentrated on Jan. Each time she played a stroke which did not earn a run, the drunks jeered. They barracked even louder when she missed the ball, and when she did run they bombarded the green meadow with comments on her arse, on her tits and on her colour.

Each comment fired more hysterical laughter and out of the laughter sprang bolder, lewder comments. A mistimed leg glide and she was to be sent back to Jamaica in a bathtub with no plug; a skied hit into the off warranted a midnight parcel through her letterbox.

As the abuse of the hecklers grew more violent, Les had fallen silent. At fifty-eight he had stopped registering Jan's score. He had placed the numbers down on the thick grass outside the boundary line. He had, it seemed—if anybody had been watching him for his reaction—lost interest in the game, even in Jan's innings.

Les's gaze was no longer on the middle. He stared at the men who had usurped his place as cheerleader, who had turned his admiring praise upside down; who had poisoned the day.

The comments hurt Jan, made the rest of the team boil. They caused George Sowerby to gather his courage and head round the boundary towards the drunks.

At sixty-nine, her concentration broken, Jan plopped up an easy catch to cover. She turned despondently towards the pavilion, yet acknowledged the warm applause for her innings from the fielding side. Their captain walked with her a few yards:

"We're ashamed. It's never happened before."

Jan heard herself saying, "It's okay, I'm used to it." It wasn't okay and she wasn't used to it. This green and pleasant land, she thought.

George Sowerby had made his protest. For his pains, he was tipped in the ditch by the departing hecklers. Next time, they promised, it would be the river. Half the Hartleywood Women stayed to comfort Jan, the rest who were not yet due to bat, ran to help George. "Just lost two buttons and my pride," he said as he returned to the pavilion, limping slightly and rubbing a bruised elbow.

"It looks as if your Glee Club's moved off too," said Ali McGuire as Jan emerged tentatively from the poor light of the changing room.

"Your lucky mascot didn't turn out so lucky after all," said Olga, opening bowler and number eleven. There was a sense of relief all round at this news, for the feeling was that if Les had not been so noisy and flamboyant in support of Hartleywood, and their opening bat in particular, none of this unpleasantness would have occurred.

To Jan, that seemed unfair. And it was puzzling: Les had not waited to give her a clap. She wondered, he couldn't have gone after them, could he?

My Sir Lancelot!

The triumphant hecklers had bought more beer. They drank it in the town centre. They were observed. They progressed down the High Street to the local Wimpy bar. They were followed. They ate and they were watched. Eventually they returned to their van parked beside the river. They drove out of town.

A country pub. Opening time. The hecklers were first in through the door of the *Fatted Calf*. Theirs was the only vehicle in the car park, and it was approached by a young man on foot. In one hand the youth carried a large box of tissues, in the other a length of plastic tubing.

Three minutes later the youth could be seen sprinting away from the van. A fire had started under the petrol tank of the van. The flames of a secondary device licked upwards towards the engine.

The blast shattered window panes, though the draught of it did not reach a solitary motor cyclist heading back to town.

★   ★   ★

The following morning the Hartleywood Women's XI were driven out of Gloucestershire and into the Marcher county of Herefordshire. They spent the morning in Hereford, and all the while Jan felt she was being observed: Les, of course.

Elaine had suggested coffee in the Cathedral precinct instead of legging it round the shops. "Yes, I feel him too. It's creepy. Do you think he's harmless?"

"Maybe he's in training for MI5."

"You've got fond of him, haven't you?"

Jan protected herself: "I scored sixty-nine yesterday, the biggest knock of my life, and he didn't clap me home."

Elaine agreed. "That was strange."

At the afternoon match, with the cathedral's pinnacled tower as a majestic backdrop, there was no sign of Les or his motorcycle. At least he's not here to distract me, thought Jan on her way to the wicket. Her second ball moved in the air and kept low, flattening her off-stump.

On the long return she gave first-wicket-down Jo Sharples an apologetic smile. "It's swinging," she said; and thought, I'm missing my Lucky Mascot.

Jo answered by glancing back at the pavilion. "We've got trouble."

Yes, trouble. Two of yesterday's hecklers had turned up in an orange-painted Renault van. They were firing questions at George Sowerby and the rest of the team.

"Sorry, we can't help," George was saying.

The taller man spoke in a temper. "In my opinion, you're not lett'n on. That lad's committed a serious crime."

Olga insisted, "He's nothing to do with us."

The shorter man welcomed Jan back to the pavilion with the words, "She'll know, Mal. Here—before you've took them pads off." He grabbed Jan's wrist, pulled her towards him from the pavilion step. "Listen!"

"Leave her alone!" Olga was brushed aside by Mal.

"We're goin' to sort this out. Let her be, Danny . . . Now start talk'n, Black Beauty."

104

"About what?"

"Your joker friend," snapped Danny. "He follows us, and he blows up our van. He could've killed the lot of us."

Mal came in, "It were you he was shout'n for."

Jan fought to stay calm. She sat down. She began to unstrap her pads. Her hands shook.

"Are you list'nin?—the lad on the bike. We want him!"

"An' don't bloody sit there like we was a couple of turds, say somethin'!"

A grim stubbornness had entered Jan's spirit. She glanced up, fiercely, but also afraid; and said nothing.

Elaine spoke for everyone. "We don't know the boy. He's not our responsibility. So why don't you just take your charming company elsewhere?"

She was taken by the shoulders and hurled sideways against Jan. The bench tippled them both over into the grass. "We mean business, lady!"

George forced himself between assaulters and assaulted. "You're angry, and quite right in the circumstances. But we really can't be of assistance to you. Naturally, if we could—"

"No we bloody wouldn't!" shouted Elaine. "Would we, Jan?" It was meant as a challenge.

Jan was back on her feet. She had picked up Excalibur. Though she held it unthreateningly, she sensed a certain confidence and strength emanate from it. "You say he blew up your van. Did you actually see him do it?"

"We seen him."

"So he walked up bold as brass while you were in the van?"

"We was in the pub."

"Sitting at the bar?"

"Yes."

"Does it look out of the window?"

"What? Does what look out the window?"

"The bar?"

"It was him!"

Another wicket had fallen—Alison, leg before while

attempting a pull off the back foot. Eleven for two: it was a bad start.

"Okay, Mal. We'll get no 'elp here." Danny shook two fingers in Jan's face. "We'll be back."

"All this hassle's doing nothing for our game," sighed wicket-keeper Renée. Then she added meaningfully, "But we all know our Les, don't we?"

Jan didn't, not in the sense Renée seemed to intend it— as if what these men alleged Les had done was far from unlikely.

"You don't really think he'd do that?" Elaine was another non-villager, shipped in from even deeper in the city jungle than Jan. "I quite liked him."

George answered for the others who knew Les. "He's a strange boy, though I like him too. There was a story went round that he set fire to his Dad's garage. Nothing was ever proved, and no charges were ever made."

Jan and Elaine clapped Alison back into the pavilion and the matter was dropped while Ali went through her usual merciless self-analysis after a failed innings. "I just didn't keep my eye on the ball. I'm certain someone was glinting something at me—straight in my eyes."

"Sun on glass, maybe," soothed the ever-sympathetic George.

"Definitely not." Ali turned to Jan. "It's that lucky mascot bloke of yours. He's in a field with binoculars." She was amused. "Honest. I don't suppose he intended to distract me, but . . ." Ali glanced at the faces around her. "What's the matter with you lot?"

It was agreed that somebody ought to warn Les Bottomley of the danger he was in, guilty or not of fire-raising. Jan went alone. That way, he might explain everything and listen to sense. She circled the elegant cricket ground to the far boundary where there was a copse of elm and beyond it pastureland. At the corner of the meadow was a cattle trough and directly behind that, a fallen tree displaying its roots to the sky.

She watched an over delivered to Elaine who was fighting to recover confidence after a run of poor innings. She clapped as Elaine tucked a short ball past leg-slip for a brisk two.

"What are you doing here?" She first spotted his feet and the wheels of his motorcycle. "Well?"

"Watching."

"Do you realise those glasses reflected the sun into our captain's face?"

"Rubbish. She simply played too late across the ball."

"And what about me?"

"I'm sorry. I got here late."

"Why—because people are after you?"

"Maybe."

"Did you do what they say?"

"What do they say?"

"That you set fire to their van."

He came out from behind the log. "They'd no right in this world treating you like that yesterday."

"Then you *did* do it?"

He pursued his line of argument. "Do you think they should get off scot-free for insulting a person like that?"

"No."

"But they would have."

"You paid them back?"

"Yes."

"On my behalf?"

"Kind of."

"What right had you to do that?"

"Who else would have done anything?"

"You could have hurt somebody."

"I was careful. If you let people get away with things, they'll do them again. I'll not stand for that."

"Just who do you think you are—Superman?" Her aggression drove him back a step. "Because you know what you've done? You've not solved the problem, you've made it worse. Not only for you, or me—but the whole team. Thanks to you, those jerks are terrorising the lot of us."

Les Bottomley concealed his feelings; they were strong, almost overwhelming, but he bottled them. "Perhaps I didn't go far enough."

Jan's anger left her. She stared at his misty green eyes which all at once seemed plunged into a deep, inner gaze. He disturbed her, but she was afraid for him. "Look, Les, I do appreciate . . . the thought. But I don't need a knight in shining armour, thanks very much."

She did not want to leave him like this. There was a bench. "Want to sit down?" She smiled. "More comfortable than a damp field."

He sat beside her, silent.

"Do you know who you remind me of, Les?—Don Quixote, riding around on his old horse charging at windmills. Only this is the twentieth century."

Les relaxed, returned her smile. "Don Quixote was attacking giants to impress his lady."

"Windmills, Les. That was the point. He *thought* they were giants."

"So those guys yesterday were windmills, eh?"

Elaine had begun to open up her shoulders. She on-drove a full-toss and the ball cracked against the iron wheel of the sightscreen.

"Great stuff!" Jan clapped hard and Les joined her. The team was recovering well.

There was a breeze off the meadow, carrying the scent of hay, and Jan began to enjoy Les's company. He talked about his mother. "She read me all the stories. And I still read them. *Don Quixote* I've read five times. I could answer Mastermind questions on it."

The mist vanished from his eyes as he spoke. "And the King Arthur stories—the Holy Grail, Sir Gawain and the Green Knight—"

"Don't tell me, let me guess your favourite." He blushed, for it was all too obvious. "Sir Lancelot, right?"

To cover his embarrassment, and forestall any mention of Queen Guinevere, he rapped out his favourites among the Viking sagas: Thor, Loki, Bragi god of poetry, his wife Iduna, keeper of the apples and Heimdall, watchman of the gods.

Jan wanted to ask more about his mother, for in everything Les said—everything he recollected—she seemed to be the inspiration; the ghostly heroine of every tale.

Instead, she laughed. "Well for me you'll always be Don Quixote." She stared at him. The attraction was very strong. "Sir Les on his faithful old Yamaha."

He laughed back. "Suzuki . . . Les the Samurai!"

The conversation ended as abruptly as Quixote's encounter with the windmills. One second Les was perched on the bench, the next he was dropping backwards like a cleanly-struck fairground coconut.

The enemy had returned, this time in force: four men in an open-topped farm Land Rover raising dust along the boundary; coming in Les Bottomley's direction.

Jan called, "Keep out of sight!"

"No use. They've seen me." He was dragging his machine towards the path. There was no way out of this meadow except back through the cricket ground.

"Your helmet, Les!"

"Look after it for me." He was away. He turned left, front wheel momentarily off the ground as he accelerated.

A bevy of home supporters scattered in panic as the Land Rover approached. They tripped over camp chairs and picnic hampers. Their shouts and waves went unheeded as the Land Rover braked dramatically in front of Jan.

"So you don't know the bastard?"

"I didn't. Now I do. And it wasn't him."

Her words were eclipsed by the vehicle pulling away. Pigeons strutting peacefully in the outfield rose in consternation as cricket was transformed to moto-cross.

For Les there was only the main exit to go for unless he

opted to crash through a fence, leap a boundary ditch four feet wide or somehow manage a route through the tennis courts.

A second vehicle belonging to the hunters of Les Bottomley—a red Cortina estate—was parked across the entrance. It contained two men.

Jan sprinted towards the pavilion. Les veered from the entrance, in his turn scattering spectators. The Land Rover was gaining, having dared to trespass on the field of play. It forced deep-mid-wicket to retreat in hefty backwards strides, and eventually fall over.

Meanwhile Renée had gone down almost on one knee. She swept a short delivery along the ground with a classic pull, appreciated by few if any of the spectators who were now in occupation of the outfield. They were darting in all directions, attempting to anticipate which way the chase would go next.

Les had no alternative but to cross the sacred turf. He circled third-man. The Land Rover followed. Third-man was so transfixed she did not dare move a limb.

The match froze. The bowler watched. The fielders watched. The umpires watched. Only Renée kept her concentration, taking up her readiness position—left shoulder facing the opposite wicket, bat resting neatly behind her lightweight boot.

The pursuit wove a mad pattern against green acres and white statues. George Sowerby was on the pavilion steps, shouting loud but unheeded threats. The Hartleywood Women's XI also raised a bristling chorus.

Jan's cry was shrillest:

"They're going to kill him!" She scooped Excalibur into the air. "We've got to stop it."

On the field, Elaine had reached the same conclusion. She stepped out of her crease. She shook her bat angrily at the Land Rover as it crossed the pitch, leaving tyre marks on the yellowed turf. "You crazy bums, get off our pitch! Get out of our lives!"

Elaine went for the Land Rover. It was reversing, planning a short-cut through gully. She swung her weapon at the despoilers of the afternoon. She hooked their radio aerial past backstop.

Suddenly the battle was on. The Hartleywood Women surged over the field armed with bats and stumps and holding pads as shields. Olga had thought to bring ammunition: three practice balls and a spare set of bails. She tossed a ball to Jan. "Aim for their windscreen!"

The infantry closed off the line between Les Bottomley and his pursuers. But the two men from the Cortina had decided to work a flanker. They strode up through deep-mid-wicket. One wielded a jack handle. The other swung a length of chain.

Momentarily Les could not decide what to do. He stopped, put down a steadying foot: was this surrender? Yet for Don Quixote such a decision had to be unthinkable.

He chose to attack, turning pursuers into pursued.

Outraged, the hunters tried a reverse ramming; missed, flattened the wickets at the bowler's end, then stalled. They watched Les swerve between outstretched wheel jack and swinging chain and head for the boundary seat where Jan had placed his helmet.

He stopped. He took time insolently to raise the helmet in salute. He waited a second as if tempting the Land Rover to follow and then rode into the deep grass of the meadow.

At a point where only his helmet was visible, Les switched off his engine. Then he ducked till there was no sight of him from the cricket field.

The driver of the Land Rover knew well enough where the prey was hiding. He screamed out of the mêlée of Hartleywood infantrywomen, almost flattening Jan's toes as he went. This was triumph. It was the Falklands War all over again, and these Argies would be crushed for ever.

He was cheered on by his comrades. He hurtled through fencing—and then, and only then, he spied the ditch. In the same desperate instant, he saw the grass-concealed plank across which Les had steered his machine.

Down went the front wheels, up bucked the rear wheels. Out pitched the flying foursome. Simultaneously Les pulled his bike upright. He sped on to the cinder track.

The rearguard of the assault force were meanwhile surrounded by a quivering arsenal of willow blades and wicket points.

"Surrender!" commanded General Alison McGuire.

Slipping through an eighteen-inch gap between the red Cortina and the gatepost at the ground entrance, Les Bottomley slowed. He looked respectably calm as he passed a police car on its way to deal with the trouble.

Sitting in the car was George Sowerby who'd run off several overweight pounds to reach a phonebox and find, to his immense relief, a police patrol car parked beside it.

George spotted Les. He was about to say something, but checked himself. Les Bottomley would meet his Waterloo in due course, George decided.

The driver of the police car glanced at Les as he passed. "Not him?"

George crossed his fingers. "Not him."

Shropshire, and cool westerlies off the Welsh mountains; a quiet game under a quiet sun, with no sign of Sir Les; only a sense of him, Jan felt. He was in her thoughts most of the time. The wind was his whisper, and the rocking motion of the trees. Straight bat, that's it. Angle this one, tickle it. And the runs came.

I'd like him to be seeing this. Batting successfully had all at once become a pleasure shared.

Yet Olga's words represented the views of the rest of the team. "Let's hope we've seen the last of him."

Only Elaine supported Les, and that out of friendship for Jan. "He's trouble, yes. But he meant well." Later she was to say, as much to herself as anyone else, "They don't make people like Les any more, do they?"

The team lodged in a guesthouse in the Cardingmill Valley. This was perched against a cliff of rock, eyeballing a mirror image of gorse and heather and vertigo-defying sheep. From the bedroom Jan shared with Elaine, the opposite face of the valley looked close enough to reach out and touch.

Below, a shallow stream slipped lazily over white pebbles. It was here, on a patch of grass beneath Jan's window, that a bivouac appeared towards dusk, and a campfire was lit. A dark form squatted in the tent entrance, feeding the fire with twigs.

"Is it him?"

"Who else?"

"His bike's not there."

"He'll have hidden it up in the bushes."

"It's creepy . . . I mean, what do you feel about it?"

Jan did not know exactly what she felt. Somewhat comforted, even a little flattered; yet strange. Uneasy. "Is it just me he's protecting, or all of us?"

"You're the one. What's he like?"

"Gentle. Really, but underneath—I'm not so sure."

"Has he asked you for a date?"

"Actually I think he'd prefer to keep his distance."

"He'll have to from now on. Those blokes won't let up."

At the match next day, Jan knew Les was watching from somewhere. It reassured her and disturbed her at the same time. Once more as she was at the wicket—Hartleywood batted last and had a total of a hundred and ninety to beat—Jan sensed the familiar counsel: eye on the ball; elbow up; keep your shots on the ground; leave that one, don't fish for it.

Her own cautionary words of advice, undoubtedly; according to her head, that is. Her feelings took a contrary view. She felt at ease with him, in a spiritual partnership; not occupied by him, not dominated, but in happy and equal union.

How could all this have happened so quickly, and with someone she scarcely knew?

Who are you?

Jan went on to her highest score, seventy-five not out. The match was won. The sunset was unforgettable; and yet she was sad because Les Bottomley had not been there to salute her achievement. More worryingly, she had stopped sensing his presence.

That night, no bivouac in the deep shadow of the fell, and no cheerful campfire. "Something's happened," she told herself, listening to her instincts. Yet she also listened to Elaine's common sense:

"He's probably had to go back home."

Would he have left without saying a word? Jan wondered.

Alone in the dark, Jan walked up the valley. It was a route which would finally scale the Long Mynd. She passed the National Trust shop and closed cafeteria on her left. She crossed over a plank bridge and followed the path until the only light was the moon almost directly above her.

She chose the left fork of the valley. In the peopleless silence, the stream chattered loudly down the conduits. The path took to the hillside. She stopped beside a hawthorn creaking in the wind, as if this was a place were they had agreed to meet.

Could this boy actually love me? She waited.

Who are you?

She discovered a seat next to the hawthorn. She sat down, restless, troubled. How different all this was from her London home, her city job in the bakery. Here was a person unrecognisable from the patterns which had formed her: a wild sort of dream had altered her.

She conjured up images of this new journey in her life, of the sun on grass, of cloud shadows, of the feel of the bat, the red rocket of the ball; and of the misty eyes of Les Bottomley clearing like the clouds as he spoke to her.

He had gone. She looked into the darkness and knew it.

The summer tour ended, with no further sighting of Jan's lucky mascot. The turmoil of city life dragged Jan out of her private thoughts and feelings: Des quarrelling with Marilyn over unpaid bills, a gang fight up the street, a stabbing outside the Asian shop on the corner; and rumours that the bakery had been taken over by another company.

"Come Saturday, Sir Les," she addressed him and herself, "I want to see you lined up on that boundary, and with a damn good explanation." For his desertion. Yes, that is how the city had made her feel about it. Blow hot, blow cold, do you? Fickle?

"He'll be there," believed Elaine reassuringly. "Go on, admit it, you're smitten."

Smitten. A funny sort of word; as if your feelings for somebody else reduced you to your knees. All Jan would say was, "I'm just irritated, that he never said cheerio."

Saturday, Hartleywood's first game after the tour, and on the way to the wicket with Alison. "There's somebody very special watching you today," said Ali. "So don't rush things."

Very special? Jan had surveyed the ground from the pavilion window. There was a bigger crowd than usual—but no Les Bottomley.

"An England selector," explained Alison, heading for the wicket-keeper's end to take first knock. "And to see you!"

Jan could not quite explain it to herself, but instead of becoming nervous at this announcement, she became indignant; not at the England selector, but at Les. Thanks a lot, Don Quixote. There's an England selector out there who thinks I'm worth a bus ride, so where are you? She reminded herself, the football season's started. Perhaps he prefers football to cricket.

Her turn to bat. If he thinks I'm no use without him and his advice, here's an answer. First ball, quick, well pitched up, on line for the middle stump. Breaking all the advice in coaching manuals, Jan went for a hook. Nobody moved as the ball zoomed safely over square-leg's head. An unstoppable four. That'll show you.

There: an insolent step back away from the wicket, and square-cutting a ball on the off stump for a long-chased three. She had a vision of Les on the terraces at Arsenal or Spurs. The next ball she chopped past slip for another four, following that with a wristy shot for two behind square-leg.

Yet beyond one vision was another, more obscure, but a truer vision, of a protective knight beside his campfire. Which was the reality?

The streetwise voice urged one vision; was the other merely that of a dreamer? You come into my life, said Streetwise, you stupid old-fashioned kid, with your crazy ideas about chivalry, and when the lady doesn't throw you her scented handkerchief you disappear like Shane into the sunset.

She had scored thirty as the battle raged in her head. Am I being unfair? Well? She suddenly felt him near. Perhaps her accusations had at last aroused him, tuned her into his thoughts. Am I wrong? Then come and explain why I'm wrong. She intended to phrase it, "come and prove it", instead, she expressed it, "come and prove yourself".

Meanwhile: two steps down the wicket, turning a well-pitched ball into a full-toss and lifting the ball back over the bowler's head. Then square across the crease, cracking the ball with such venom that the fielder at deep mid-wicket applauded the four rather than reaching out a boot to prevent it.

This was the first century scored by a Hartleywood player since Ali McGuire's club record knock of a hundred and five four seasons ago.

Okay, does that impress you? If so, where are you? A four to long-on; another past point; two more through the gaps from which fielders had just been moved.

At first Jan had been reluctant to be singled out by the photographer from the local weekly paper. "It's a team game," she had protested. Then she had changed her mind: if Les happened to see her picture, it might remind him that she still existed.

Course, do *you* exist any more?

The question banished her anger. It alarmed her sufficiently to make her decide against catching the early train home.

Instead she accepted a lift from Alison and an invitation to celebrate in the *Fox and Hounds*.

There was a jug of ale on the house and the England selector gave Jan warm praise. "I couldn't recommend you more highly, my dear. Are there cricketers in your family?"

Jan laughed. If only you knew my family. She shook her head. A moment later, she felt George's hand under her elbow. "See the character nodding at you? That's Les Bottomley's dad. He wants a word with you. The lad's gone missing."

Mr Bottomley was already on his way round the bar. Gruff and without any introduction, he said, "You seen him?—our Les."

George tried to help out: "This is Mr Bottomley, Jan—"

"He done a bunk, as per usual when there's jobs on. Lazy little sod."

"When?" she heard herself ask.

"Two week nearly. They say he were soft on you, come round watching, like."

She remembered the day, but was not given time to mention it. "Did he tell you anything?"

"We talked, but not about him—"

"It's that bike I'm worried about too. He could've had it stole."

"You think that would have made him run away, Mr Bottomley?" Jan was as desperate—in a different way—to find a reason for Les's disappearance as his father.

"And he's shoved off wi' two 'undred quid."

"Stolen?" came in George.

"His own, which his mam left him. But gone, the lot." Mr Bottomley was looking for someone to blame. He had lost his wife. Business was bad, as bad as his relations with his son. He was lonely, hurt, bitter. Now he had lost his son altogether. "Was you stringin' him along?" he asked Jan. "Women twist our Les round their little finger." He paused.

He looked for support to George. "But never a Black before."

There was an acid silence until Jan decided she would speak up for her missing friend. "We just talked. He was kind and intelligent and—"

"Intelligent? What you talkin' about? He was remedial. Backward as a snail." He was half away. "What you do other than play cricket?"

Here was someone, Jan decided, who would always snatch at the wrong end of every stick. But she answered. "I work in a bakery."

To Mr Bottomley, this proved his point. "Huh." He broke the air with a barking laugh. "Two snails together, then!"

Home. The bakery. Six till four, overnight Thursday. Beginning once more to suffocate under the monotony. Then, to the amazement of all, the announcement of Jan's selection for the third Test against the touring Australians.

It was in the local paper; even in the national tabloids. Jan posed for pictures in the bakery yard, holding Excalibur in various batting positions, though she felt the photographers were more interested in her legs than the accuracy of her square-cuts, hooks and on-drives.

If Les had run away to London he would surely notice the press coverage. She hoped he would ring, write her a note. She thought, he needs all this as much as I do. She wanted to share the fame and attention with him.

She told Elaine at the last Hartleywood match before the Test, "If I could explain his absence, I'd let the whole matter go out of my mind. But I can't."

News of Jan's selection for the national women's XI had multiplied the average attendance at Hartleywood. George Sowerby was delighted. "Today's collection will pay for the new pavilion steps."

Forthwith, Jan was out in the third over, leg before wicket. Serves me right. Back in the pavilion, after the usual comradely commiserations—that the ball would have bounced a mile above the stumps, that the umpire had no right to give a person out who'd stepped down the wicket (and Jan had surely done that, everybody agreed)—Jan sat alone with her thoughts.

This is ridiculous. I feel him watching me. His voice is in my head. It's a haunting. Of her innings, she thought, "I didn't seem to care."

What's your opinion, Sir Les?

It would have hit the wicket.

What did I do wrong?

You know what you did wrong.

Went neither forward nor back, right?

Right. So you don't need me.

Football, is it? Or another girl?

What do you think?

You haven't left me any options.

Elaine stuck her head round the pavilion door. "Somebody to see you." For a second of joy, Jan thought it was Les. "It's that Neil, Les's pal."

"Oh." She got up, surprised at the power of her disappointment, yet intrigued by what news Neil might have of Les.

He stood nervously on the verandah, face in shadow. It was to be bad news. He cleared his throat, grinned. "Congratulations! Les said you were the best . . . You've proved him right."

She waited. Neil was holding a newspaper, tightly folded. He handed it to her. "We're not sure if it's him." He cleared his throat again. "But it's possible, like."

The newspaper was a Shropshire weekly. There was a front page photograph of policemen in a forest clearing. The headline read:

BODY OF YOUTH FOUND IN WOODS

Jan stepped into the light. Her hands trembled as she held the paper. An unnamed youth had been buried in a shallow grave, said the report. He had been horribly beaten, and stripped of his clothes. So far, the police had no lead as to who killed the youth or why.

Neil answered the first question in Jan's mind: "His dad's been up. Says it's not Les. But they'll find out, from his teeth or something. We just thought you ought to know." He turned. "It's not certain. I mean, if his dad . . . His own son, like." He ended with a question. "Eh?"

She did not speak. She returned the paper. She stared into Neil, into the motive in his eyes. She offered him nothing to tell his friends, except her silence; and her distance.

It was her way.

If Jan Rickards was to have a chance of being selected for the winter tour of Sri Lanka, she had to make a good impression quickly, and her chance had come with England's winning the toss and electing to bat.

She had no shortage of support. A luxury coach had brought villagers from Hartleywood. The Hartleywood Women's XI were all there, and George Sowerby stoutly distending his Hertfordshire blazer. They cheered the BROWN BAKER FROM BRIXTON as the *Daily Mirror* described Jan. She took the field with Kent's Audrey Baines, in the *Mirror*'s opinion "Women's answer to Stonewall Geoffrey Boycott".

Never suffered nerves like this. How do you bat when your hands are shaking like leaves in a gale, your legs wobbling all over the place, your eyes won't focus and you're breathing like you've just climbed Tower Bridge?

"Concentrate on the ball," George had urged. "Nothing but the ball. And remember—bat and pad close together so you don't let anything through the gate."

She hadn't slept. She had spent the dark hours mentally rehearsing strokes, visualising crowds, counting fielders, anticipating short deliveries, checking her instinct to step out and hurl her temper at the ball.

And that silly inner voice persisted: you'll be batting for your sex, for your colour and for your class. Stuff and bloody nonsense, it's for myself.

Your ego.

All right, all right, my ego.

And him, Sir Les of the Windmills?

In the news, there had been nothing. She had rung Les's dad. "I've nothing more to say than I've told the police, and the papers." He had put down the phone.

Why are you worrying? A father ought to know his son. Yet if they had beaten him beyond recognition, taken his bike, burnt his camping gear?

They?

The men who chased him. Who else?

I shall go up. Make the trip when this is over; to the ground by the river. He didn't let them get away with it. You owe it to him. To be sure. Elaine will come with me. We'll go to the pubs. We'll—

What?

Run them to earth.

You and whose army?

Me. He was my friend.

Person unknown.

It had been a relief not to face the first ball; even more of a relief to have Stonewall Audrey Baines pat each delivery back up the wicket. Yet now it was Jan's turn, and her head was spluttering and crackling with advice.

Take it steady. Don't waft at balls outside the off stump. Watch that chip shot off your legs and for God's sake don't hook until your eye's well in.

She took guard, scratched a guideline with her left foot, made a blockhole and closed feet and bat into her textbook left-shoulder-forward stance.

You can do it.

Les?

You can do it. You're wonderful.

Have you been tilting at windmills lately?

You're Queen of the Willow, and don't forget it.

Her fingers tightened around the handle of Excalibur. The ball was well wide of the off stump.

This one's for you.

Jan raised the bat high and brought it down in a crashing curve. The fielder at point, who had been brought in close for Jan's first over, leapt out of the way of a shot which would have broken her shin.

Applause. Four all the way.

What did I tell you?

Where have you been? Where are you?

You're the best.

Jan turned the next two balls calmly to leg, drove the fourth for a two and shuffled the next off her legs.

One to go.

Where are you?

Silence.

She looked into the sun. Her gaze went past the bowler who was commencing her run. On the rim of the ground at a spot midway between mid-off and cover, Jan saw someone wave: it seemed to be a wave. She saw a youth on a motorcycle; on the handlebar, a red helmet.

Les!

She saw his red helmet but not the ball. She hesitated, letting her bat stray from the safe proximity of her pads—and the ball shot straight through the gate and into the wickets, raising from the fielders a jubilant chorus of celebration.

Then the long walk; bitterly disappointed, yet her heart thumping at the vision which had distracted her. It's him. Jan could not see that angle of the ground as she returned to the pavilion. She stared ahead of her, acknowledging a "Bad luck, Jan" from first-wicket-down.

So you turned up after all?

She could not explain what she felt; it was a mixture of sunshine and thunder. She went up the pavilion steps to a roar of sympathy from Hartleywood, and calls of "Chin up!" and "There's always a second innings!"

Yes, always a second innings.

She stripped off her batting gloves and pads. She went out of the back entrance of the pavilion, down steps, past the little print shop which would already be recording her paltry six runs for posterity.

From a hundred yards away, Jan knew the motorcyclist was not Les Bottomley. She halted, eyes momentarily incapable of shifting from where they had rested—on the red helmet that belonged to somebody else.

I should have known: you'd never have tried to distract me, would you?

Silence.

She was recognised by spectators. They were kind. "Don't worry, pet, that was a great four!" And a question, "Did the sun get in your eyes?"

She turned in the direction of the voice. The movement of her head dislodged a tear; two tears, each mingling with the sun to distort her vision.

The questioner was waiting for an answer. Jan tried to smile. You have to, you're a celebrity now. "Something like that," she said. It did not seem enough. Now she did smile as a tear slipped down her face.

"You see," she added, "I lost my lucky mascot."

Those were the words Jan almost said, but they were too private and they might not be the truth.

You are alone, and you are strong. "No excuses," she said. "That's what happens when you don't play down the line of the ball."

Next time it would be different.

Right, Les?

Right.

The Rebellion of the Names

For the very first time in the experience of anyone in the Company, the Director came from behind his desk. He seemed very much taller than usual. He thrust his ivory mask-like face so close to that of old Charlie Bentley that it cast a crooked shadow across the bridge of his nose.

Nor did the Director often shout. It was rarely necessary. All that was needed in this modern organisation was a whisper, and people jumped to it. But the Director shouted now:

"Mr Bentley, I hold you utterly and absolutely responsible for that boy's conduct."

In danger of swallowing his tongue, Charlie Bentley stumbled, "I only . . ."

"You only?" interrupted the Director, his ivory mask tinged with the kind of purple which characterises the inner recesses of the artichoke. "You only? You call it only? *It* only? There is no confounded 'only' about it. You're fired, as of now. Better still, of yesterday."

"But sir, the boy—"

"Out!"

"I was only supposed to train him."

The Director's phone rang. He would have preferred to have crushed Charlie Bentley with his fist instead of lifting the receiver. However, he had been expecting—no, fearing—the call.

It was the Chairman of the Company. The Director seemed to have shrunk in height. "Yes sir—but sir! . . . It was only . . . No sir, I don't dare call it 'only'. Utterly and absolutely, yes sir."

The Director replaced the phone. His mask had become

as green as the outer leaves of the artichoke. He stared at Charlie Bentley, once his most trusted deputy, faithful servant of the Service the Company rendered its clients. He listened to Charlie's plea of mitigation:

"It wasn't our fault, Director."

"Charlie—you're finished, I'm finished, our part in this noble Enterprise at an end. Utterly." A hand rose to shrivel up his mask. "And absolutely."

Ramsey, Boulting, Lear, Atkinson, Kirk, Rivers, Hutchison, Cliff, Peters, Hirst. The names landed in Gary Farnworth's sleep like the nuclear artillery in a video game between East and West. Scammell, Dawkins, Kinsey, Davies, Crabtree, Wallace, Robinson, Williams. Loads of them. Endless. In his dream, Gary counted the Ms. There'd been Muddy, a Mudd, a Millichip as well as boring old Mason, Miller and Mann.

Yesterday had been full of Ws. Waterson, Willingshed, Wattles, even a Waffen as well as the usual dross of Wilson, Waites, West and Warren.

It was boring. BORING. There'd never been a job from the beginning of time, not to mention before the beginning of time, which was so utterly boring. So absolutely boring.

Monday: "You're a very lucky young man, Gary. This job had two hundred and eighty-four applicants, including a Doctor of Philosophy, twenty-seven BSCs and sixty-eight arts degrees."

"Then how come, Mr Bentley," Gary had asked, "that I got the job with only one Grade C GCSE, in Woodwork?"

Mr Bentley grinned. He was too busy and too old to give an honest answer. "Because you were the only one to wipe your feet before entering."

Boring.

"An interesting occupation."

Boring is my experience.

"Which may lead to a fine career."

Like yours, Charlie?

"I beg your pardon?"
"Thanks very much, sir."
"You may call me Charlie."
I'll never end up like you, Charlie. Never.
"These days, when jobs are gold dust."
Yes, Charlie, no Charlie.
"Three bags full?"
"Sorry, sir?"
"I thought you said Three Bags Full."
"Never said anything, Mr Bentley."
"Well you don't go getting cheeky."

Three Bags Full Farnworth. How did I get that name; and what does it mean?

"Three Bags Full means, Farnworth," said Gary's House Master the day he left school, "that you nod your Long Kesh, alias Upper Belson, alias Ripe for the Guillotine head when it suits you, and do just what you like when it suits you."

Yes sirs, no sirs, Three Bags Full, sirs.

Bullock, Curtis, Hitchcock (him too? I thought he was dead), Merrydown, Fawcett, Longman, Plumb, Lemming —could anybody actually be called Lemming?

"Lemming, Mr Bentley? Isn't that the animal that all of a sudden panics and throws itself off a cliff with its kith and kin?"

Kith and kin? A strange boy for sure, decided Charlie Bentley. He had reported it to the Director. "The lad seems to be almost educated, sir. Yet we asked for somebody without qualifications."

In a philosophical mood, the Director answered, "The present generation pick up bits of knowledge like your thieving magpie collects broken glass and silver paper. Fortunately they don't make any more sense of it than the magpie does."

As to the original question, Charlie Bentley confessed he was unfamiliar with the habits of self-extermination attributed to lemmings. "It takes all sorts," he said. "In any case, my boy, it is not your task to query the names."

"Query them, Mr Bentley?"

"Well, think about them. They're just names. Think of them as blanks."

"But how am I to get through the day without—"

"Take an old hand's advice, son."

"Which is?"

"Forget they're names. That's the first rule of the job. The names are nothing to do with you or me. When the List comes down from Top Office, simply go to the card index. Simply look up the names alphabetically. Simply extract the cards appropriate to the names. Simply carry the cards to the Desk. That is all. Job done."

And naturally the other way round. When the cards are returned, simply take them to the shelves. Miles and miles of them, Mr Bentley. Yes, Gary, you could lay our cards at sixty centimetre intervals and step from here to Sarawak and back.

Simplicity itself. Take it out. Replace it. Read the list. Take the list to the files. Down dark corridors, dark avenues, dark boulevards. Smell the rotting cardboard. Use the stool if necessary. It's on castors.

Remember?

Yes, Mr Bentley?

You just forget your Lemmings.

Tuesday there'd been a Starbuck. Liked that name, did Gary. Better than Star Wars. Perhaps there'd be a Mr Starwars. Also liked Wigzell, Pender-Cudlip, Percorini, Jinks (Hi, Jinks. Yes, laughed at that one; and Hunnable —how do people get such names?).

Wednesday, and Gary forgot all about names when he met Julie Deacy from Top Office. "Deacy?" he asked, "Where did you get a name like that?" It ought to be Monroe: not quite as ravishing, not quite as blonde, but at least the hair was natural; not as shapely, either, but you could call her subtle. And down here in the eternal twilight, with only the smell of cardboard to keep you company,

any shape resembling *that* shape was worth the whole alphabet put together.

Fact is, Gary Farnworth had become obsessed with names. There'd been a Card. There'd been a Company. There'd been a Shape. There'd been a Worth. And of course, a Monroe.

To Charlie Bentley he had declared, "I'm going to become the World Champion in Names. They'll put me in the Guinness Book of Records."

Charlie had not understood him. "How do you mean, World Champion?"

Gary wasn't quite sure what he meant either; but it helped him cement his relationship with Julie. Or it could well have been the other way round, for she had asked, with a vulnerable smile not unlike that of Monroe, "You're the world expert in names, I believe?"

Julie no more understood what being the world expert in names meant than did Gary, but it kind of made them both feel important. "One day you'll be a celebrity."

He had returned her smile, though his was a Gary Cooper smile, masterly but lopsided. "I put it all down to teamwork," he drawled. He offered his hand. She surprised him by taking it.

"Deacy by name," she said. "Deacy by nature."

Gary laughed. "You don't mean dicey, do you?"

"It means just what you want it to mean."

He wondered for a second whether she was crazy. After all, everybody else in this place was crazy. He said, "Will you go out with me sometime?"

Julie Deacy frowned. "Permanent Staff are not permitted to date Temps, at least not on the premises."

"I'm a Temp?"

"Cardboys are always Temps in the Company."

"You mean after seven days they're like the Lemmings, join their kith and kin and rush off the white cliffs of Dover?"

"Nobody sticks the job for long."

"Suppose they did?"

She was apologetically coy. "They're got rid of. Surplus to requirements." He looked crestfallen. Julie judged him brighter than the usual; and he was not unlike another Gary she fancied once. "I'll tell you what. If you're at the bus stop first left at five-thirty-five, I'll give you another answer if you want to ask the same question. How about that?"

He did. And she did. And it was all arranged: Gary Plus Julie Equals Okay.

Names. Gary recognised that his head was becoming like one of those ornamental glass balls which you turn upside down to cause a snowstorm. A blizzard of names. Dainty, Primm, Weekly, Dinkum—Dinkum, was that possible? Couldn't a Dinkum have a name-change? Burlipp, Pitkin, Nutter—Nutter? Are people bats to have names like that? He looked for Barmy, and found it; on the way to it, he found Badlad and Baldman.

He pictured them as two undercover agents patrolling the shishkebabs of Basra. Wednesday he brought his roller skates, determined not only to be the World Names Champion but the Roller-Disco World Names Champion.

Charlie Bentley chided him: "This isn't the playground, Gary."

"You want the names, Mr Bentley, you get them twice as fast."

During lunchtime in the park, Julie Deacy refused to give Gary a kiss until he had removed his roller skates. "It's not dignified kissing a boy wearing skates."

"That's because it makes me so much taller."

"No, it's because you keep slippering about."

Like an Eel. Like a Fish. Like a Troutman.

When they had finished their sandwiches and shared Julie's flask of coffee, Gary asked a question which earned an unexpectedly abrupt reply:

"What happens, Julie?"

"Happens?"

"With all the names?"

"We process them, of course."

"That's what old Charlie said."

"Good. So now you know. More coffee?"

Gary sipped a silent coffee and watched Julie's averted face. He was remembering his conversation with Charlie who had, first off, said, "Anything you want to know, my boy, don't hesitate to ask."

So Gary had asked: "Mr Bentley, what happens with the cards?"

Charlie had looked as blank as Julie. "Well, son, the cards are processed." The old man had stared into his tea as though some names had got in there by accident. "That's about the long and short of it."

"What I mean is, Mr Bentley, when you ask me to go and get the cards—"

"Sorry, factual error, my boy. *I* do not ask you to get the cards. I merely pass on the order from Up Top."

Gary agreed to take matters one by one. "You having passed on the order from Up Top, and me having done what Up Top requested you to request me to do—what actually happens to the cards?"

"They're taken Up Top."

"Yes? And then?"

"And then they are returned."

"But Up Top," persisted Gary, "what do they do with the cards?"

Charlie paused, tea to lips. "Why," he said, peering over his bifocals, "they process them."

"*They* being Julie?"

And this is where Julie Deacy had protested. "I do no such thing. I do not process the cards. That's not my job."

"Don't be angry."

"I'm not." She was furious. "It's not me. My job is to follow instructions."

Gary was intrigued. He could not control his curiosity. "You don't process them, but you follow instructions."

"Yes. Now can we go?" Her knees flashed as she got up. He did not want to lose her.

"All I wanted to know—"

"Listen? Do you want this job?"

He gazed at her fiery lips. He was in love, partly because everything was a mystery. "Now I do."

"Then do it, and keep your trap shut."

Upset, Gary trailed after her. It was Stormly. There was comfort in names, yet he felt Brown, going on Black. She was all Stride. He couldn't Turner.

"Julie!"

Come Monday, and cards to find a place for; crisp cards, newly typed, fresh-smelling. Touched by Julie's scented fingers, Gary imagined.

Everybody cheerful. "We're expanding!" rejoiced Charlie Bentley. He pushed a stack of newcomers across the counter towards Gary. "Find them a home, Gary boy. It's all cash in the bank."

"You want them processed, Mr Bentley?"

"Processed?" The word was a bit of a Tees on Gary's part; to Charlie, it was Holly, right up his Crutchley. "You," he hurled, "don't process nothing! Understand?"

Gary was learning Guile (yes, there had been a Guile on Friday, as well as a Guillemot). "That's a big job, is it? the processing."

Charlie felt he had been something of a Harding on the boy. No need to be Short with him simply because he was rather Green. He was thus a modicum more forthcoming: "The Process is a Process upon which rests, it can be argued, the health of this dear nation of ours."

Charlie supped and spoke: "Pride, my son, that is what we all feel in the Company. In our unique service."

Gary looked at the cards in his hand. He had no answers. "We offer a Service, Mr Bentley?"

"Wright."

Gary was very much into pursuing this line of enquiry,

when a Card Out, which had become a Card In, caught his eye. Gary Farnworth scanned the card and sensed a shock-wave close in on his heart: he knew this person.

Fact is, the person on the card was Gary Farnworth's step-father. The card read:

CROFT, Michael, Alan.

Mick to his friends, but Gary had volunteered to call him Dad. He was worth it.

Dad, you're famous.

I'll tell him tonight. It'll cheer him up.

"But that kind of thing," continued Charlie, unabated, "mustn't be divulged to a living soul outside these four walls, mind. Remember the Three Monkeys?"

Dad, this is your card.

These cards are real people.

"See no evil, hear no evil and speak no evil. You got my message, boy?"

Boy, that wasn't so friendly. Charlie had his nasty side. He wagged his finger with it.

Gary waited till Charlie had retired to his desk piled with Cards In and Cards Out. He waited with a strangely beating heart, as though he had done something wrong and was about to be found out.

Till now, the gaze in Gary's eyes had been like Charlie's description of the typical British workman: inert. A good word; quite surprising coming from Charlie: "Inert, that's what they are. The only energy they expend from Monday to Friday is to stuff their pay packet in their pocket."

Till now, Gary had been inert. What he was told to do, he did. Fetch a card, he fetched it. Return a card, he returned it.

But this was his dad's card: CROFT, Michael, Alan.

It had never occurred to him to read any of the thousands of cards Gary had 'processed' during his first week with the Company. Cards are cards. They are boring. Almost as boring as names. Everybody has one.

"My job," Julie had said, "is to fill them in. That's all."

"Fill them in with what?" Gary remembered himself asking.

"With details."

That, for the present, had been sufficient for Gary. Now, having slipped between the rows as if to pull at an illicit fag or check the boobs on page three of Charlie's rag, Gary took notice of the details of his father's card:

CROFT, Michael, Alan.

Site Engineer.

Details correct.

Or were partially correct, for Dad had not been a real site engineer for at least five years. He had lost his job when the firm had been taken over; and he'd never managed to get another one.

Funny that, what with all his qualifications.

"My face doesn't fit, Gary."

"How do they know it doesn't, Dad, if they don't give you an interview?"

Dad didn't know. Eventually he started knowing even less. He began to wither. There wasn't much of him left.

"Fact is," confessed Gary to Julie, "my dad's dead. I talk of him in the present because I can't stand the thought . . ."

"The thought?"

Names: Knight, Walker, Bridge, Waters, Graves, Court, Case, Payne and Pain and Paine.

Winter.

"I'm sorry."

"Got over it."

Gary read his dad's card. The further details were as unexpected as walking into your front room and finding it occupied by armed men in masks. He read it over; and over.

Dad never told me this.

About the knife at school. Stolen. Containing two ordinary blades, one long and one short, a hacksaw, a corkscrew and a flat-ended multi-purpose blade. About the insolence to masters: once called a lady teacher a 'silly bitch'.

Went straight. Did training. Qualified. No further reference to knife with two ordinary blades, one long and one short, etcetera.

Then came the xs. Joined the xxxx political party. Recruited to xxxx trade union. Became xxx official. Subscribed to xxx periodical. Took part in xxx dispute. Led xxx protest. Joined xxx organisation. Went on xxx march.

All these xs amounted to a Recommendation:

"Potential troublemaker; probably subversive. Not recommended."

Gary approached Charlie's desk. He asked, in a still, shocked voice: "What does xxx mean, Mr Bentley?"

"You been looking at the cards, young man?"

"No, but there being all these xs, I just couldn't—"

"Don't read the cards, boy. Don't worry about the xs. Let *us* worry about them."

"Are they a code?"

"A code? Oh, yes, a code."

"The opposite of ticks, are they? Like in school?"

"Ticks? We don't have no ticks. Just xs."

Gary turned, indicated the Hall of the Cards; or as Charlie preferred to call it, the City of the Cards. "Then all these people are bad?"

"Bad?" Charlie removed the crook from his back, puffed out his yellow tie. "Nothing like that." He paused, thought carefully. "There's good and there's bad."

Gary waited, then asked: "Do you have a card, Charlie?"

"Of course not."

"Do I?"

Charlie laughed. "Not yet, son."

"How do I get a card?"

"Too many questions, Director—the lad'll have to go, I think."

"Very well, Charlie." The Director put on his Sadd look, his Vicary look, his Moody Head Teacher 'I've-been-badly-let-down' look. "I thought this Government

Training Scheme guaranteed us Non-Thinking Personnel."

"That's what we asked for, sir."

"What's the lad's name again?"

"Farnworth, sir."

"Do we have any Farnworths?"

"Hundreds, sir. Plus Fletchers, Faiths, Fallons, Flemming's Frenches, Fuggles and Fulkers ... We're particularly strong at the moment in Fs."

"But we got nothing on his family?"

"Always check these things with new recruits, Director. We've a Farnworth who lives in the next street but one. No connection."

The Director asked what sort of questions Gary Farnworth had been posing.

"What we mean by processing; and about the xs."

The Director had a sense of humour. "Tell him they're kisses—and then get shot of him, quick."

"Yes, Director."

"Oh, and Charlie—"

"Sir?"

"See that there's a card filled out on him."

Gary met Julie in the park after work and told her the bad news.

"I've been given a week's notice."

"I know," replied Julie calmly. "You started reading the cards. That's breaking the Golden Rule."

"But *you* type them."

"The difference is that I don't *think* of them." She smiled sweetly. "Typists are like that. As far as they're concerned, they could be typing toasted muffins, not words."

"What if you saw your own card one day, or your dad's?" She was silent and he persisted. "The truth is, you do know what's on those cards. You just pretend you don't know."

This was their first row. It was going to be painful,

but it was delicious making it up afterwards. First the row:

"I don't want to talk about it."

"You don't want to talk about it because you know it's wrong."

"I don't know what *it* is."

"Yes you do. *It* is keeping cards on people without them knowing."

"I don't know that."

"You don't know what?"

"That they don't know."

"Well I've been reading the cards, and what's on them is nasty. It's bad news. It's dishing the dirt. And if people knew—"

"They're just records."

"Then why do they go in and out—to give them exercise?"

"I don't know."

"Yes you do."

Julie changed tack. "We give a service. And it's perfectly legal."

"But wrong?"

"How can it be wrong if it's legal?"

Julie had broken away. She stood under the trees and watched a couple of Muscovy ducks glide across the lake. "Why can't we just forget work and enjoy ourselves?" He was silent now and did not persist. She felt she was losing him. "You ask too much," she said. Yet she had become fond of Gary, and just a little bit proud of him for asking all those questions—questions her own mind had entertained earlier in her job.

She turned to face him. "My mum's a widow, you know. Gets paid less than me." She tried some advice on him. "These days if you want to hold on to your job, Gary, you keep your mouth shut."

"All I want to know, Julie, is how the Company can make hundreds of quid—"

"Thousands—"

"Thousands of quid just keeping cards on people." He waited, but she was putting distance between them, over the bridge and home. As if in sympathy, the ducks too had parted company, one towards a screen of willow, the other towards the weir.

"Right then," he thought.

Gary's mother usually got in late from work on a Tuesday. He left her a note, 'Gone to the pub'. He went with a screwdriver. Thick woollen gloves. A balaclava. Dark sports shoes with deep-cut rubber soles.

Names: Wall, Pipe, Scales, Tough, Armstrong, Leapman, Knott, Roper, Land, Casement, Lock, Tapp, Mew, Catt, Send, Clinch.

Into the City of Cards. You let me down, Julie, so this is what I'm having to do. Cocking, yes. A Snook. Shelves like tower blocks. Gary no longer saw cards but people, hundreds—thousands of them, their personal details ticking away like time-bombs. He flashed his torch down the streets of the city.

In a whisper, he addressed the names: "What have you lot done wrong?"

There was a card on Dad.

Dad could never get a job.

There must be a connection somewhere.

Gary had never been allowed up the stairs from the City of Cards. There was a notice above the wrought-iron balustrade: ACCESS ONLY TO AUTHORISED PERSONNEL. Even Charlie Bentley wasn't permitted further than the reception area to the Director's office, and only then when he was escorted by the Director's secretary.

Up there and beyond were what Charlie once referred to as the Specials. "People with degrees," he said. "And that."

"Where the cards are processed, Mr Bentley?"

Ignoring Gary's persistence, Charlie continued, "They

come in by a private entrance, up a private staircase. That's how special the Specials are."

"Something to do with the Government, are they, Mr Bentley?"

Charlie never listened. "Up and up and up," he said; and that was a kind of answer. "And out and out and out." His eyes were moist. "The States, Japan, West Germany, Cape Town, wherever . . . Wherever they want . . ." He had tailed off.

"Names, Mr Bentley?"

Julie and Gary had made it up. Very passionately on the back seat of a number eighty-eight bus. He did not tell her of his plans, but she suspected him of something or other. "You'd not think," she mused, "they'd be so careless as to leave the keys to everything under the secretary to the Director's orthopaedic cushion. Would you?"

Inspired by Julie's collusion, Gary tiptoed up carpeted stairs, past a lonely yucca plant to an open-plan office whose luxury would have done credit to the pages of the Office Equipment Review. He found the keys. Julie had said, "The smallest operates the Director's dictating machine."

Later, he decided. His eyes were on the next floor, tempted by the notice, STRICTLY AND ABSOLUTELY FORBIDDEN TO UNAUTHORISED PERSONNEL.

Up and up, out and out.

He had scarcely reached the landing when instinct drove him bellysmack to ground. Footsteps from below. A torchlight probing the stairwell. Gary peered through the foliate iron as the nightwatchman ("Watch out for the nightwatchman," Julie had warned) swayed up from the darkness. He was drunk.

"Poor little neglected creature!" The nightwatchman had paused at the stairs corner, addressing the yucca plant. "Too busy to give you a drinky-poos, are they, the lousy swine? Then here goes." The yucca was treated not only to illumination but to liquid refreshment. "That's better, my old midnight friend. Ha! Ha! A relief to us both."

Gary stared down on the nightwatchmen's bald head. He listened to a rather one-sided conversation. "You're quiet, this evenin', darlin'." A laugh, or was it a heavy sob? "What's up—they got a card out on you, eh? They decided you're a subversive yucca? Been writing to the papers, have you? Been seen wearing naughty badges? Come on, you can tell me? Who you been meeting?

"Is it Shell as been asking after you? Are they thinking twice about having you in the foyer of British Telecom? Is it Harrods want the dope, Selfridges, Sainsburys, Safeways, Sutton Seeds; is it P & O, RTZ, Cash & Carry; is it oil or the buses or the trains, British Aerospace; is it your Barclay Card gone dicky? Have they stopped listening to you at the Listening Bank?

"Who wants to know, me old red yucca? Because it's in them cards. One word from them and you'll never see another office windersill in a thousand year."

The nightwatchman had moved out of Gary's view. He was at the secretary's desk, on the swivel chair which did not so much squeak as fart, gently and with decorum. At first Gary thought the nightwatchman was impersonating the Director's voice:

"Do me a letter first thing in the morning, Miss Geranium."

Geranium? Gary wondered whether her Christian name was Rose or Daisy or Marigold.

"Yes, Mister Director, Sir, Your Lordship." This was the nightwatchman for real, in dulcet soprano.

The Director's tape-recorded instruction issued forth without interruption, save for the occasional grunt:

"We've received a request from headhunters Morpeth and Rigby, to have a name deleted from our records. I've said to them, Once On, Never Off; but they claim their client has been . . . that he is in the clear. Spotless. I've checked. They're absolutely right, of course. I must have a word with the Specials not to exaggerate. There are eleven errors of fact on the man's record according to Morpeth and Rigby.

"Nevertheless . . . striking off is definitely not Company policy. Even if the facts on a person are wrong, the very existence of a card on him or her must be proof that *something* is wrong. Am I right?"

The nightwatchman answered for the absent Miss Geranium:

"Yes, right, my Lordship."

"I mean, it's like the law, isn't it? If the law kept admitting it was wrong—who'd have any trust in it any more? Same with our records. When your multinational corporation checks with us about a potential recruit, they expect to find there's something wrong. A spotless record would be bad news. They'd have wasted their fee. Am I right, Miss Geranium?"

"Absolutely, Your Sultanship."

"It follows that if the Company says a thing is true, that is exactly what it is . . . Even if, in strictly factual terms, it isn't. Am I right, Miss Geranium?"

"Indubitably, your infallible Popeship!"

"However, Morpeth and Rigby rank among our best customers. Their client, it turns out, is a true blue down the line anti-communist church-going freemason whose one and only wife does meals on wheels for the elderly and whose children are members of the Pony Club of Great Britain.

"Our record that he is an undercover agent for the anarchist anti-vivisection feminist league union of shop stewards dedicated to the subversion of British commercial enterprise is, therefore, at fault."

"But only marginally, Your Eminence," answered the baldheaded drunken Miss Geranium supportively.

"My decision, in consequence, is to agree to the withdrawal from our records of the offending card. Delete the name, Miss Geranium, and add that of a newcomer rather more suitable for our lists."

"Instantly, Your Hallowed Graciousness."

"In return, I am asking Morpeth and Rigby for a dozen new names to take the place of that which has been deleted. I think that is fair, don't you, Miss Geranium?"

"A gold top bargain, oh Wise Head of the Ages."

"I knew you'd agree with me . . . Oh by the way, I want that yucca plant removed. I get the feeling it is watching me."

The nightwatchman switched off the tape. For a moment he was silent. Then his voice seemed to slide up the beam of his torch as he trained it on the door through which only the Specials were permitted to pass.

"And who am I, lads? King Kong? Winnie the Pooh? Mr Jeremy Fisher?"

He descended the stairs. He paused. He whispered and the whisper almost amounted to an echo:

"Rumpelstiltskin is my name!"

Gary felt a twinge of pity for Charlie Bentley who had gone down with summer flu. Oh dear, what a shame; leaving Gary under the supervision of—nobody.

He had learnt enough to decide. To decide was to act. There was little time. The names awaited him. He got to work.

Abbas was invited out first, and immediately after, the Abbits, the Abbots (two hundred and sixty-six of them), the Astles, the Attwaters and the Ayres. They took a card-walk. Some visited Crust, Cuckoo, Cullumbine and Culpepper who themselves were destined for elevenses with at least five hundred Halls and around the same number of Hammonds.

At school Gary had always felt sorry for people at the end of the alphabet because they got read out last, and were always last in the queue to tell their Weekend or Holiday News, by which time nobody was listening.

He invited the stuvwxyzs to muscle in among the three hundred and fifty or so Bakers, which led the Bakkers,

Bakowskis and Balaams not to mention eight hundred Balls to take a morning dip with the Ms.

Cooks went West; Fairweathers joined the Hills among the Lanes; the Lesters went to Bradford; the Birminghams to London; the Lewises to Derbyshire; the Kents to Avon, while the Brittans went French.

The Muttons joined the Lambs; the Matthews teamed up with the Marks, Lukes and Johns; Masters got their Children; Keats got his Milton and Parsons joined the Churches.

Gary thought, everything is beginning to make sense. So intent was he upon his labours he failed to notice that, as he paired Salmon with Fish, Sales with Moneypenny, Sweeney with Todd, Crook with Hook, Robbins with Hood, Bacon with Egglestone, Trundle with Sprint, Chuck with Thrower—as he worked this labour of love, he was being observed.

"What are you doing, Gary Farnworth?" queried Julie Deacy. The look of accusation on her face indicated that last night on the bus was last night on the bus. She was back at work. She had reverted.

"Sorting the cards, Julie," he answered lamely, his hand containing Postlethwaite about to disturb the deep purple calm of the aristocratic Le Bas, Le Beau, Le Besque and Le Breully. He had turned Scarlet.

"Sorting is not your job."

"But Julie!"

"Don't you but-Julie me." The evidence was before her. She reached down a box of Gs. After Gale came Storm; where Gardener should have been was Plumber; where there should have been Giles there was Miles; for Glazier, Grazier, for Gower, Power, for Grace, Race.

"Look at it this way," said Gary seizing a bold initiative. "You can always put these names on a computer, then there'll be no problem about getting the cards in order."

It was a trap and Julie, in her state of shock at the ruination of the work of a decade, stepped into it. "We can't put names on a computer. Then the whole thing would have to be licensed . . . Declared to the authorities."

"And to the people in the cards?"

"Very probably."

"So you can only keep this information as long as it's on cardboard?" Oh dear, what a pity, he was thinking.

She was Steel, with or without an 'e'. There was to be no more Larkin. He was out of Luck. She was going to be Noble. If he'd expected Perks he was to end up Loveless; up a Pole without a Paddell.

He said, "That's me, then, is it—a Rowland Stone that gathers no Moss?"

Julie stared at Gary as if she had all at once realised that he had lost his senses. It must have been the cards, hour in, hour out, day after day; and she decided, it's a kind of nervous breakdown. He's not really responsible for his actions.

At last the springs in Julie's Hart began to work in Gary's favour. She was Fuller of compassion than she could Bell Eve. She suddenly felt a Long Inge to take his Head into her Hands and kiss him.

Julie Deacy did just that. And then her arms Took over. His body was Slim and Supple, but no Stringfellow he; there was Bull in his embrace; there were Lyons in his loins.

And the shelves shook, the cards Fell; the names tumbled like the leaves which sheltered the babes in the Wood. All the beautiful names, the Peasmarshes, Clovers, Goathursts; down came Flood and Lavender, Toltree, Merlin, Badger, Ducket, Malpass and Nottage.

By afternoon teatime, Gary and Julie were engaged.

When Charlie Bentley returned to work from his bout of flu, the City of the Cards, the Nation of the Cards, the Universe of the Cards, was strangely silent.

"Boy?"

Gary Farnworth did not answer to Boy.

"Son?"

He did not answer to Son. He wasn't any man's son.

Nor had Charlie been greeted as usual to the cordial smile of Miss Deacy, though a pile of request slips, done immaculately on her IBM, stood on her desk, impatient for action.

Charlie (as per Company instructions) never read the cards, paid no heed to names. On this particular morning, when he should really have stayed off for another week to recuperate, he was in no mood to go beyond the bounds of duty.

He picked up the top request slip which sought information on an applicant for the post of chief executive of an animated film company, one Donald Duck of Buckingham Palace, Sunset Boulevard, Peking.

"D-d-a—no, u-c—C for Charlie—k, k for kerbstone which is what I'll be hitting that Farnworth boy with when he turns up. DUCK."

Charlie pulled out the cardbox marked DU. "D for—Shakespeare?"

In his tracks, he stopped. Must be the flu. Still dizzy. Or these new glasses, for the names were advancing on him, crowding him; jostling: Napoleon Bonaparte, Kamikazi Corner, Pyramids Avenue, St Helens. William the Conqueror, Nightstop, Rio de Janeiro. Genghis Khan, The Falls Road, Volgograd. The Queen of Sheba, Arc de Triomphe, Cleethorpes.

They were stampeding him. His flailing arms brought down cards. His elbows brought down cards. His hip crashed cards. Where had the sudden draught come from, the wind that lifted white-flickering card-clouds up into the dank air, in spirals, in pirouettes, in forked lightnings?

Julius Caesar, Greta Garbo, Rin Tin Tin, Thomas à Becket, Florence Nightingale, Ku Klux Klan, Dracula, the Bishop of Bath & Wells, George Washington, Lady Godiva (Scotch Wool Shop, Coventry), James Bond, Ivan the Terrible (Toad Hall, Never Never Land); all of them denying on the grave of their mothers, on the tombs of their forefathers, that they had ever been Members of the Pixies' Afternoon Tea Party.

Ivan the Terrible spoke for one and all: I massacred millions, but I never joined a union!

Old Charlie surrendered under the weight of the names. They carried him out and administered oxygen and soothed him as he spoke like an avalanche of how he had been viciously mugged by a load of Bs who'd gone in with a wrongful assembly of Fs who'd not watched their Ps and Qs. "It's a rebellion!" cried Charlie. "We should call in the army."

Meanwhile, for a short time at least, the Hall of the Cards was strangely peaceful, at one with itself. The cards seemed to enjoy being out of order. The Ls talked with the Rs, the Ds with the Gs, the Is with the Us. Being so few of them, the Xs, after generations of neglect and misuse, were made a fuss of.

"You know, Gary," said Julie Deacy as they sat watching the ducks in the park, "we've not really achieved anything much. We've only delayed things."

He knew what she meant. Soon all the cards would be back in order. They might even send down some Specials to speed up the operation. "You reckon we should have burnt them?"

Julie watched the ducks paddling upstream, the breeze rippling their feathers. "I'm still thinking about it."

Only one card was missing from the Hall of Cards. "Here's a start," commented Gary. He held up the card. The flame from his match licked hungrily at the card, curling it, browning it, obliterating its contents.

The card was that of: CROFT, Michael, Alan.

The Great Tattoo

It was never Big Steve's intention to get into a whole lot of trouble. Admittedly he looked trouble. He was beefy. In the dark he could suddenly loom up like a pantechnicon reversing down a one-way street.

Yet his girl friend Louise always said Big Steve was Mister Gentle. His only fault—if you could call it that—was his pride. Bears are like that. They give you no trouble till you prod them. Louise was convinced, "Our Steve's just a big cuddly bear who got prodded." Meaning that in the normal course of events he would never have set fire to anything, much less a whole row of houses.

Of course the prosecution in court repeatedly asked, "What if there'd been people in those houses next to the shop in question?" At which the defending solicitor had said that there weren't any people in the houses next to the shop in question.

But what if there *had* been?

The houses, persisted Defence, were condemned. They were too horrible even for rats to live in.

The magistrates nevertheless, in Louise's view, and in the view of Big Steve's Mam, Dad, three brothers and two sisters, had their perceptions coloured by this big But If.

But Ifs shouldn't come into it, argued the solicitor for the defence.

The image persisted: it could have been murder; mass murder, even. And naturally the magistrates didn't particularly like the look of Big Steve. Not with his skull shaved to the nobbles and his zebra-lined black leather jacket clinking with gallantry medals of the First and Second

World Wars, swapped for a complete set of Manchester United programmes for the 1973–74 season.

Big Steve did not help matters by his demeanour. He never raised his eyes to questions from Prosecution or from the bench and there seemed to be only three words in his vocabulary:

"Don't know nothing."

Big Steve was like that. Being something of a bear, he was averse to prodding; being also a human, he perceived questions as prods with a sharp stick. "Don't know nothing."

"Your trouble, Steve," Louise had once said, "is that you say the opposite of what you mean. If you don't know nothing it means you know something. Which means people think you're trying to hide something, right?"

Big Steve had replied, "I never try to hide nothing."

Louise had given him a triumphant punch below the ribs. "Exactly!"

As Louise predicted they would, the magistrates presumed that when Steve said he didn't know nothing about the fire started in the basement of Tattoos Unlimited, he meant the opposite: he did know something.

Louise guessed that Big Steve had misunderstood the question. He knew about the fire. What he didn't know nothing about was why he started it.

She had been unable to help. She loved his slow eyes and flappy ears, but even ears that size could not pick up a whisper from the public gallery where she sat with Big Steve's Mam, Dad, three brothers, two sisters, grandparents on his Mam's side and his twin aunts, Evie and Belle.

"Don't say nothing," Big Steve's dad had advised him. Louise had kept silent.

"If he don't say nothing," cautioned Steve's mam, "what'll the judge think?"

Big Steve's dad expelled an impatient sigh. "He'll think he don't know nothing, stupid. Which'll mean he didn't do nothing."

If only, thought Louise, life was that easy.

Sure enough Big Steve had followed his dad's advice, said he didn't know nothing about the fire, that he'd not done nothing. And sure enough the magistrates found him guilty of arson, namely by setting light to old newspapers in the basement waiting room of Tattoos Unlimited, proprietor Mr Dene (without an 'a') Oakman.

Additionally the magistrates agreed Big Steve was responsible for the spray-canned message on the exterior wall of the company. This was direct, appropriate and in impeccable language:

FLAMING CHEATS.

What chiefly entertained Louise's mind before and during the trial was an unresolved question: why get so worked up over a simple spelling error?

Now, Big Steve was without doubt a respecter of many things. He respected, or rather revered, motorcycles. He respected animals. His Great Dane, named Mugsy after the jazzplayer Mugsy Spanier, was better cared for than an oil sheik in a private patients' hospital. And Big Steve respected jazz. Not your Top Ten, your Who or your David Bowie, but your golden oldies New Orleans style, with their hot lips round tenor saxes and their flashing trombones.

He would listen with half-closed lids to musicians his pals—and Louise—had never heard of; and usually never wanted to hear of again: Peanuts Hucko, Gene Krupa, Tyree Glenn, Ziggy Elman, Peewee Russell.

He was, under the spell of jazz, another person. Louise had told her boss about Big Steve's respect for jazz. "Your boyfriend," said her boss, "strikes me as a bit of an eccentric. Does he play himself?"

Louise had laughed. Big Steve had a respect for her laugh. "No, he plays the drums."

To complete the list, Steve respected all things soccer;

rugby league; cage birds; his dad's prize leeks; his mam's meat and potato pie—and Louise's superior education (as well as her face and various parts of her person).

What Big Steve did not respect, or so it would seem, was the English language. He didn't speak it right. He didn't spell it right—except for his message on the wall at Tattoos Unlimited.

This had not bothered Louise till now. Seeing her boyfriend in the dock, and a holiday with him to the Isle of Man about to be ruined, helped focus her attention on a contradiction: if Big Steve had so little respect for the English language, why should he burn the tattooist's place to the ground just because Oaky had got one puny letter wrong? Not even a wrong letter; merely the right letter in the wrong order?

It didn't make sense.

(In any case, she mused, who would ever see the letters in the wrong order, considering his chest was covered up with a shirt eleven and three-quarter months of the year?)

(Or would he feel ashamed of it in the Isle of Man?)

Not mentioned so far in the list of Things Big Steve Respected was the local chapter of the Hell's Angels, called the Vikings; in rivalry with their early English counterparts over the canal, called the Saxons.

This was another bit about Steve Louise could not understand. Greater even than his ambition to cause a sensation at the Newport Jazz Festival with a drum solo lasting five hours, was his dream of being invited to become a fully-fledged member of the Viking Chapter.

Every indicator was that Steve was suitable material: his bike—faultless; five hundred ccs of British-made galvanised turbo energy; his gear and regalia—boots, guards, jacket, skids, jinglers, skenners, skull-trap—superb.

Rock, Chieftain of the Vikings, had long given Big Steve hope of admission to the Holy of Holies. "You're qualified," he'd said. "More or less."

By qualified, Rock had not meant the number of educational certificates Steve had obtained (or actually not obtained). One such certificate would have disbarred Steve for ever. That's what made the Chapter suspicious of Louise. It had got round about her certificate in typing and shorthand.

"She's enemy," pronounced Kirk, Sub-Chieftain in the Chapter's early-night rendezvous, the *Hanging Man*. "We don't want no upwardly mobile bints riding pillion with this outfit."

"Since when," came back Rock, "did we judge a bloke by his bint? Big Steve's qualified. Done his test. Got his hassle with the stripes. Mixed his cocktail with the Saxons. We got to keep to the rules, man."

Kirk stood his ground. He laid his gauntlet between jugs of Newcastle Brown. "He'll not prove to my satisfaction he's one of us till he makes a choice. The Chapter or the bint."

Rock gave Kirk a look. He felt the shadow of Kirk. Kirk was second in command. The rest of the Chapter was looking at him—Rock—and it was looking at Kirk. It was a kind of test, for Kirk was ambitious as well as being five inches taller than Rock.

(Hadn't Kirk been reported as murmuring, "Oh yeah, the Chieftain is as hard as rock—Blackpool Rock"?)

Rock played it cool. "Since when has a bloke had to chose between Chapter and his bunker?"

Kirk was sharp. "Very rare, Rock. And only when a bloke's bunker is persona nod grafta. You get my meaning?"

Rock didn't have an exam pass in Latin, but the persona nod grafta (or persona non grata as the dictionary variation has it, meaning unacceptable person) sounded like it was not exactly a come-on. And true, this Louise bird had a bad habit of speaking out of turn. She had opinions. When you tried to shout her down she came back with arguments and facts and words like persona nod grafta which made you feel a bloody idiot.

Kirk regarded himself as the brains of the Chapter. He impressed everybody but Louise, which was why Rock had a soft spot for her. Just the same, Rock sensed that the Chapter veered to Kirk's position. Aware that it is usually the leader's privilege to hijack other people's ideas and employ them as his own, Rock said, "Big Steve has still something to prove. Let trial commence!"

"What's your opinion on tattoos, Lou?" Big Steve had asked her, following his interview with the assembled Vikings in the car park of the *Hunted Fox* off the Oldham Road.

"You're stuck with them for life, that's what I think."

"Because I've decided to have one."

"*You've* decided?" Louise had sensed the drift of things. She was tempted to argue her case, but decided against it. Big Steve was rarely swayed by argument. His mam never stopped arguing with him and invariably she made him more determined to go ahead with his plans than if she had merely answered, "Your choice, son, you're over eighteen."

Louise had read how in Soviet prisons inmates had had their foreheads tattooed with insults to the State. Very bold statements. And unremovable. Which meant that they walked around insulting the State for the rest of their lives. Unless, of course, the State condemned them to have their heads removed.

"Where?" she asked with pretended indifference.

"Down Sudell Road."

"No." She was patient. "Where on your person?"

He proudly drew his hand across his chest.

"All of it?"

"Right across."

"You've a hairy chest."

"I'll have it shaved."

"It'll grow again."

"I'll shave it again."

Louise had never cared for tattoos. Her dad had 'Lorna' tattooed down his forearm. He had divorced Lorna and Shirley, his latest woman, resented waking up in the mornings with Lorna written right beside her.

Steve knew Louise disapproved. Kirk had said as much. Steve had joked, "So long as it's spelt right." They had all laughed.

"Tattoos Unlimited is the best," approved Rock. "My cousin Oaky will do it personal. The best."

Louise had been firm on one thing, "Well you just leave my name off your chest."

"No sweat, Lou."

This meant the message was already decided. Louise could not keep a note of sarcasm out of her voice:

"What's it going to say—'I LOVE PAGE THREE?'"

"Don't be crude. The Chapter's decided. It's going to say—HELL'S ANGELS FOR EVER." He grinned, full of innocence and delight. With those four mighty words on his chest he would be a blood-brother of the Vikings. History would have been made.

Big Steve would have arrived.

Respected.

Privileged.

In.

Louise had been profoundly depressed. "That's it, isn't it? *In* is all you've ever wanted to be." If Big Steve had been looking into Louise's face he would have been prompted to offer comfort. But his eyes were dazzled by the words shortly to be emblazoned on his chest.

"Where do I come in?" he heard her ask.

"You'll be okay. You can ride pillion. They said—"

"On condition—"

"Yeah, on condition—"

"That you go and do what I'd not want you to do, right?"

He was honest. Bone honest. He hung his head slightly. "Right."

Tattoos Unlimited had formerly been a Greek kebab takeaway. The local authority had taken away the customers and rehoused them in what most of the residents believed was even worse accommodation than that which they had left.

They also missed their kebabs.

There were still casual visitors who entered the tattoo shop asking for doner kebab with or without onions. The story goes around that a Norwegian seaman emerged with SHISH KEBAB indelibly inscribed on both arms, though actual proof of this has been difficult to obtain.

For the average client of Tattoos Unlimited and its self-styled 'Artist of the Needle', Rock's cousin Oaky, an appointment to be written on for ever was special. For Big Steve it was like a christening.

He was very proud. "You'll be chuffed to death," Oaky had promised him. "You've got imperial purple inside regal red with royal gold edging. You've acanthus leaf trimmings at the foot of each down-stroke and a bayleaf cluster on the final R. It's a masterpiece. Blow out your chest, Steve, and stun the world!"

On leaving Tattoos Unlimited and meeting Louise after work, Steve refused to unbutton his shirt and permit her a glimpse. She had laughed good-humouredly. "Oh, it's covered by the Official Secrets Act, is it?"

He beamed. "Something like that."

"Does that mean you're going to unveil yourself?"

"Unveil myself? Do you mean strip off?"

"No, like they unveil a monument or a plaque?"

He had nodded, pleased with the thought. "It'll be in front of the Chapter. They'll be first to set eyes on it. A real ceremony, like."

"Don't tell me you've not had a quick peek at it in the mirror."

Big Steve didn't often score one over his girl Louise. "You seen letters in a mirror, Lou?" He half throttled her with his right hand, in the friendliest and most affectionate manner. "The letters is about-face, stupid!"

Louise had never thought of that. With a careful eye she gauged Steve's line of vision from stretched neck to inflated chest. "Fact is," she said, "you'll not be able to see your own great tattoo. Except upside down and at a terrible angle."

Steve had not thought of that either. He was silent, troubled, then the truth flushed through his face. "Course, it i'nt for me to read, but other folks."

"Ah, like a sandwich board." She couldn't resist it. "SHOP AT TESCO."

Before he could get angry, Louise made it up to him. "It's easy, we can hold up one mirror to your chest and another mirror to the first mirror." She paused. She was no scientist. "Would that work?" She relaxed. "Better still, I'll take a photo of you, get it enlarged and reproduced on a tee shirt or something so you can sport your letters even on a cold day."

Friday is the night when most things happen and it was the evening Big Steve was to reveal The Great Tattoo to his comrades in the Viking Chapter of the Hell's Angels. "It's probably the greatest day of my life," he told Louise. She had not been too happy with this comment, for he had always said the greatest day of his life was meeting her.

She had replied, "You mean *the* greatest?"

He got the hint. He was not insensitive. "Meeting you, Lou, was private, like. This is . . . er, public."

It was as gracious as Big Steve was ever going to get so Louise let the matter pass. Men were all too understandable, she thought. A hug in the dark is the most wonderful thing in the world—until, that is, you get the chance to show off to your mates. "Anyway, I hope it all goes well. I'll be at my sister's."

The entire Viking Chapter of twenty-nine (the maximum permissible being thirty) were present around and about the pool table and bar of the appropriately chosen hostelry, the *Flag Unfurled*. News of The Great Tattoo had spread among the estates, that Oaky had excelled his own much-trumpeted virtuoso technicianship.

Oaky claimed, "What I've done for Big Steve will rank among the Thirteen Wonders of the World, and will make the Hanging Gardens of Babylon look like my back yard."

Naturally, being an artist by choice and a boaster by nature, Oaky had gone over the top: "What's more, that tattoo will be considered part of the national heritage. When Big Steve dies they'll have him stuffed and mounted in the Whitworth Art Gallery. They'll have to stick the Pre-Raphaelites in the basement to make way for him."

Another rumour had gone round that Oaky had charged Steve enough to keep the poor lad in debt to the turn of the century.

Big Steve entered the *Flag Unfurled* to applause. It was a giddy sound. No one had ever clapped Big Steve before.

He had arrived.

Respected.

Privileged.

In.

Or almost in. They assembled before him like the whole United squad doing their pre-season photo-call. Some squatted, some knelt, some wedged themselves on the red plastic seating and against the wall-length mirror engraved with THWAITES ALES. The unsteady perchers propped themselves up with billiard cues.

Rock took charge of ceremonies. He conducted a brief Chapter prayer—to Woden, God of Motorcycles (Rock knew his Viking sagas from back to front). Then came the unveiling. Kirk received Big Steve's jacket, so heavy it needed two taut biceps to prevent it crashing to the floor. Then Kirk removed Steve's Thor God of War scarf, in United colours.

"Un-button!" Rock commanded. Kirk unclasped the

candidate's top button. He stood back for Rock to undo all the rest save one.

It was the privilege of the candidate to release the final button and open his shirt like it was the stage at the Blackpool Winter Gardens. With quivering pride, Big Steve revealed his chest to the world; at least to the world that mattered—the Viking Chapter.

There was a cheer. A short one; a cheer cut short as the assembly read Oaky's work of art. And then somebody pointed, somebody laughed. They all looked along the pointing finger. It picked out the letters in imperial purple and regal red.

Rock blinked in controlled dignity.

Kirk put his hand to his mouth. He was giggling, not almost but actually.

They were *all* giggling.

Big Steve smiled half a smile. Then he looked down at his chest, already sprouting new black hairs through the upside down letters.

They were more than giggling, they were laughing. Soon they were doubled up, falling over each other, all wheeling elbows and knee-sag, their voices coming out in hoots and squeaks and squeals.

Rock silenced them. He had his cousin's honour to think about. "Cool it!" he roared. Then he shrugged and made things worse by saying, "What's a spelling mistake between friends?"

This comment was read as a signal from the Lord of the Chapter for the Vikings to laugh as some—probably all—had never laughed in their lives before.

But Steve's crest was all-fallen. While his comrades drowned in their own laughter, he sank in confusion, alone unable to share the joke. The realisation of this for Big Steve, Mr Proud, was paraffin to the bonfire.

He put his hand to his face. It was not there. He had lost it. He tore his jacket from Kirk, ignored Rock's call, "Hang on, Steve, it's only . . ." and stormed from the *Flag*

Unfurled with his shirt so tightly held across his chest that it tore at the arms.

He burst in on Louise and her married sister. "If one of yous laughs, I'll kill you to within an inch of your life, so help me!" He switched off the television. He turned on the main light. He stood before them.

Louise saw that his face was greasy with tears.

He opened his shirt front. "Read it!" he ordered.

Louise's sister came to within an inch of her life. She read and she turned away. In a choked voice she said, "I think the baby's waked up."

"Read it!"

Having seen the tears, Louise was far from laughing. But she was not going to be hurried. "It seems okay to me," she replied. "Very clever." It was tough trying to be casual for she could hear her sister stifling a giggle on her way upstairs.

"Then why're they all laughin' like drains, Lou?"

He was quieter. She could handle him. She was glad and he was grateful. "It's just that," she began, then faltered.

"Just that what?"

Louise could hear her sister up on the bed. She could picture her with her face crammed into a pillow, trying not to wake the baby. She could not stall things any longer. "There're . . . a couple of letters out of place. It hardly matters."

"'Ardly matters?" Now he was hysterical. "At the price I had to pay, you say it 'ardly matters? Christ, what bloody letters?"

Louise read out The Great Tattoo for Big Steve. "It says—"

HELLS ANGIES FOR EVER.

"Okay?"

The volcano started deep down, only a rumble at first. "It sez what?"

"Hells Angles For Ever,"

"Angles?"

"Well, yes. It's easily done, getting the L and the E in the wrong order."

The eruption was more than half way out. "Hells Angles!" Big Steve's ears were bunged up with the laughter of the Viking Chapter.

Louise tried what she could. "Who'll notice, Steve?"

The volcano burst. "They all noticed! Their 'eads fell off laughin'." His great humiliation was sinking in. His great humiliation was spreading. It was ten tons of wettened yeast in a confined space.

Louise knew there would be no way of comforting him, but she had to try. "Who'll ever see it?" She gave him a tender smile. "Apart from me, that is." She suspected her tactic might be working. "After all, you hate swimming. You never sunbathe." She thought a small laugh might be appropriate. "In fact I've only seen you once without your vest on."

Big Steve rejected consolation. "You're missin' t'point, Lou." The volcano had reversed itself. It had cooled to ice and was slipping back into the dark mountain, there to form impenetrable layers of gloom. "'Owever much I cover myself up—*they* know. They'll never stop laughin'. Ev'ry time they looks at me, they'll be lookin' through me jacket, through me shirt. Understand? HELLS ANGLES FOR EVER. For ever!

"It's a tattoo, pet. That means for ever!"

In sending Big Steve down for three months, the chairman of the magistrates had concluded his summing up with a comment which was to win him an approving headline in the local paper. He said, "I cannot for the life of me begin to comprehend how so trivial a matter as a misspelt tattoo could induce a young man of previously unblemished character to perpetrate such a reckless, foolhardy and dangerous act as burning down the premises of Tattoos Unlimited.

"That it was not this youth's intention to conflagrate the entire row of houses—happily for him and the community, empty of persons—is hardly the point."

The magistrate had turned directly to address Big Steve. "You have disgraced yourself, your family, your friends and your fiancée."

At this reference to herself, Louise found herself rising to her feet. She had lived these last weeks in torment. Their holiday on the Isle of Man was a puff of smoke on the horizon. Their engagement plans all off ("You'd not want to marry a wally, Lou, and that's how I'll always come over from now on").

And what's more, Steve couldn't stand confined spaces: how'd he cope in a remand home with bars on the windows and guards at the gate?

Louise was mad at a lot of things; at everything and everyone, practically, except Steve. Yet she was not in a surrendering mood.

She was on her feet and declaring, "I don't think he's a disgrace. Far from it. In fact, he's done everybody a service."

The silence was of the sort which would follow the sudden arrival of venomous snakes in the centre of the courtroom.

But for her unusually neat and attractive appearance, Louise would have been ejected into the summer rain for this interruption. She answered the unspoken question, "Because he's stood up for the English language." She had not thought of saying that. It just came out. And her comment caused amusement. The magistrates passed from one to the other the faintest of smiles.

No, she wouldn't have Big Steve go down scowling; not beaten like that; like a wet dog dismissed into the yard.

What's more, Louise had something to tell Steve. All he needed, she hoped, was something to grab hold of. To take down with him. Turn over in his mind. A straw in the wind would be enough, knowing him.

She had got him to look at her. That was a start. And on their first visiting hour she'd tell him that among the warriors of Old England there weren't just Vikings and Saxons; there were Jutes—and there were Angles.

She knew because she loved him, Big Steve had the imagination to see that the Angles had been much neglected. Why should the Vikings get all the publicity?

It might work. It might just work.

Because Louise did not sit down when requested, she was invited to leave the court. Her eyes were on Steve. Go on, go on—smile. She settled for the beginning of one.

Louise also had her pride. At the swing doors, she turned to the court, though her words were for Steve alone.

She shouted, clear and resonant:

"HELLS ANGLES FOR EVER!"